GW00854712

This book

Cillian o' Broin

Children's
POOLBEG

belongs to

Brogeen and The Green Shoes

First published 1953 by
Burke Publishing Co.
This edition published 1989 by
Poolbeg Press Ltd. Knocksedan House,
Swords, Co. Dublin, Ireland.

© The estate of Patricia Lynch 1989

ISBN 1 85371 051 2

All rights reserved. No part of this publication may be
reproduced or transmitted in any form or by any means,
electronic or mechanical, including photography,
recording, or any information storage or retrieval
system, without permission in writing from the
publisher. The book is sold subject to the condition that
it shall not, by way of trade or otherwise be lent, re-sold
or otherwise circulated without the publisher's prior
consent in any form of binding or cover other than that
in which it is published and without a similar condition
including this condition being imposed on the
subsequent purchaser.

Cover design by Pomphrey Associates
Typeset by Print-Forme,
62 Santry Close, Dublin 9.
Printed by The Guernsey Press Ltd.,
Vale, Guernsey, Channel Islands.

Brogeen and The Green Shoes

Patricia Lynch

Children's
POOLBEG

Contents

Chapter		Page

1

Where Brogeen belonged

rogeen was a leprechaun, one of the fairy shoemakers, and he lived in the Fort of Sheen, close beside the Slieve Mish Mountains, in the Kingdom of Kerry.

It wasn't easy to find the Fort unless you belonged, or were invited. You might go there in dreams, you might follow a strange tune, or forget where you really should be going and find yourself inside. If you weren't welcome you wouldn't stay long. Of course, Brogeen belonged, so he had nothing to bother about.

The Fort was one of the gateways to Tir na nOg—the Land of Youth. If you travel that far it isn't only youth you'd find, but most other things people long for.

Brogeen went journeying there now and again for a holiday or to learn how the very best shoes are made. He was a clever workman, but there's always more to know. Sometimes he went the other way, through the big door, which looks like a rock outside, to the world where we live.

When he returned to the Fort from the Land of Youth, Brogeen was always discontented. When he came home from the ordinary world of human beings he was indeed thankful. Yet he was always willing to be off again.

"It's grand to be home!" he'd say, the moment the Keeper of the Door let him in. "You folks don't know how lucky you are!"

"'Tis a pity you don't stay where you belong, if you have such a wish for Sheen," growled the grumpy Keeper. "I'm sick and tired of opening and closing for you!"

"Sure, a leprechaun must have a change!" protested Brogeen.

"I'm a leprechaun!" retorted the Keeper. "Do I ever ask for a change?"

"Old Stick-in-the-Fort!" muttered Brogeen rudely, pushing past. "You never go anywhere!"

He was ashamed the next moment. He was so happy to be back he determined he would never leave Sheen again—never! Never!

Then he settled down to work and, for a

while, to be a model to the young leprechauns who were only beginning to learn their trade, and to older ones as well.

One day he was thinking of the Land of Youth and its wonders. There was no end to them and he'd seen only a few.

"I'd love to ride a horse that would travel across the waves as easy as along a grassy path," he said to himself. "The one I heard of with a silver mane and tail sweeping the ground."

He laid down his hammer.

"It went under the sea too, and if I grew tired of that, why wouldn't I whistle for a winged horse and race the clouds?"

The leprechaun lifted his hammer as a cluricaun, with a red face and still redder hair standing up straight on his head, came racing through the Fort.

"Brogeen! Brogeen! Have you heard the news?"

"Don't be screeching and roaring and I trying to finish a job. I'm off to Tir na nOg!"

The cluricaun turned a somersault and sat cross-legged at the leprechaun's feet.

"You won't be running off to Tir na nOg when you hear the news. There'll be too much work to do."

Brogeen looked severe.

"What's this great news?"

"You remember the Princess from the Knockmealdown Mountains who was here for Bailtainne, when the bonfires were alight on the mountains for Midsummer Eve?"

Brogeen smiled.

"Is it the little one with the long dark hair and blue eyes, and a lovely pair of silver shoes, only I'd have made them a trifle higher in the heel, is that the one?"

The cluricaun turned another somersault.

"That's the one! That's the one! She's going to marry a Merman from below the Cliffs of Moher and the Queen has asked them here for the wedding!"

Brogeen flung down his hammer in a temper.

"Why wasn't I told?" he demanded.

The cluricaun jumped to his feet.

"I'm telling you now! You're the first I've told. Of course you're the first. I was sent to tell you at once. You'll be making the Queen's new shoes for the wedding. Lucky Brogeen!"

Off he went, head over heels, head over heels, down the long room and out through an arch.

2

No Shoemakers

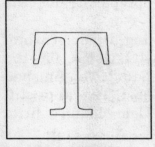ap! Tap!" went the little
gold hammer.
"Tap! Tap! Tap! quick-
er and quicker.

"Ow! Me thumb!"

The hammer went up in the air and Brogeen
put his thumb into his mouth.

"I don't care if I never hammer in another
nail!" he cried wrathfully.

"I don't care if I never make another shoe!"
he said as loudly as he could, kicking away his
last, made of white polished wood.

Frightened by his own daring, he peeped
over his shoulder and there stood the Queen of
the Fort, gazing sorrowfully at him.

"Oh, Brogeen!" she said.

"S-sure I d-d-didn't mean a word of it!" he
stuttered.

"Maybe you didn't, but I'm afraid you did,

just for the moment," she told him.

The Queen wasn't wearing her crown, for dinner wouldn't be laid for another hour and there weren't many visitors at Sheen. Everyone was at home preparing for the wedding.

Brogeen had been making a pair of white satin sandals, with pearl buckles, for the Queen to wear at the wedding. The finished one stood on the window seat. The other still sat upside-down on the leprechaun's little last.

"Are they very troublesome?" she asked kindly.

"I'm ashamed of meself!" declared Brogeen. "How could making shoes for Your Majesty be a trouble? I'll not stir until they're both ready. You'll be able to dance the whole night long without being tired."

"That will be wonderful!" smiled the Queen.

Brogeen set to work again. A second time he hit his thumb with the hammer. As he screamed with pain the Chief Harper came by on his way to the banqueting hall.

"What an ugly sound!" he exclaimed.

"If one of your strings snapped in your face, you'd make an ugly sound!" cried Brogeen indignantly.

Two fairy who boys followed the harper, one carrying his carved chair, the other the harp, stared at the leprechaun in horror.

"Who cares what two young lads think!" he muttered defiantly.

Yet he knew it was no way to talk to a grand musician.

The harper stood silent. Brogeen wouldn't look at him.

"S-sure I d-d-didn't mean a word of it!" he stuttered.

"Didn't you?" asked the old musician. "Not one word?"

Brogeen sat considering.

"I did mean it, every word of it, but only for the moment. I'd made up me mind to take a holiday. There's a white horse I want to ride— maybe you've seen it—with a silver mane and a long tail and it can understand every word you say!"

"In Tir na nOg there are many such horses!" the harper told him. "Have patience!"

He beckoned the boys. They gathered up the stones they had been tossing and rolling. One shouldered the harp. The other carried the carved ebony chair.

Brogeen took up a handful of golden nails, when along came the King, with the Queen's crown under his arm. He had caught it up in mistake for his own and was looking for her to make an exchange, though his crown was already on his head.

"What's wrong? What's the trouble?" he demanded.

"Nothing at all, your Majesty. Nothing at all!" answered Brogeen standing up respectfully. "I was doing a small bit of thinking."

"Thinking!" exclaimed the King bitterly. "If you knew the amount of thinking I have to do, you'd be sorry for me. Do you know what's happened now?"

Brogeen shook his head.

The King drew nearer and spoke in a whisper behind his hand.

"The invitations to the Good People of the Macgillycuddy Reeks and the Knocknaskagh mountains have all been returned. Not one of them is coming to the wedding—not one!"

"Why not?" asked the leprechaun in amazement.

The King spoke so softly it was lucky the leprechaun had extra good hearing.

"They haven't a decent shoe among them. Would you believe it—there's not a leprechaun for miles in those parts? And I'm being blamed! They patch their shoes for ordinary running about. But they're ashamed to be seen at a ball in them."

"You'd pity them!" sighed Brogeen, picking up his hammer and balancing it on his knuckles.

The King walked on. Suddenly he turned and came back.

"Brogeen! Couldn't we spare one of your assistants? You've taught them all you know, haven't you?"

The leprechaun put his head on one side.

"Nearly all, not quite, your Majesty. There's the Queen's shoes!"

The King nodded.

"I know! I know! She won't have them made by anyone but you. Yet 'tisn't her shoes are the trouble! Think of those unfortunates from the Macgillycuddy Reeks to the Knocknaskagh mountains not able to come to a dance. Who should we send, Brogeen? We must do something!"

"First I'll finish this sandal," said Brogeen.

He began to hammer.

"Stop! Stop!" cried the King. "I've a headache. You're making it worse!"

"I must finish this sandal!" said the leprechaun obstinately.

The King was angry. He snatched the hammer from the little shoemaker.

"You'll listen to me!" he shouted. "I'm the King, aren't I? The shoe can wait!"

"Excuse me, your Majesty!" and Brogeen took back the hammer. "I must finish my work before I leave the Fort!"

The King was so upset he let go the Queen's crown. Luckily the leprechaun caught it before it reached the floor.

"Leave the Fort!" exclaimed the King. "Don't talk nonsense! We're in a fix! We can't spare you! The Queen won't hear of it! You can't go!"

Brogeen tapped away. The more the King scolded, the faster the leprechaun worked. At last he drew back, lifted the sandal from the last, made the buckle fast and placed it beside the other.

"Now we can talk sense!" said the leprechaun proudly.

"Aren't you very full of yourself!" exclaimed the King.

"I'm only wanting to help," protested Brogeen. "Now, whatever we do, we can't make new shoes for that crowd in time for the wedding. But we must see them righted. 'Twould be a disgrace on the leprechauns of

Ireland if we let them pass up a wedding!"

"How about my disgrace!" demanded the King. "And the Queen! 'Twas she asked the Princess and the Merman to come here!"

"I'll tell you what we can do," said the leprechaun. "We'll hunt out all the shoes that weren't quite all they might be, we'll gather the ones that are always being poked away because they're too good or not good enough. The Good People of the country will be at that wedding. There'll be only one missing!"

"One!" said the King. "What harm! Who'll miss one?"

The leprechaun glared at him.

"Didn't I tell you who that one will be?"

"I wasn't listening," yawned the King. "Tell me again. I'm listening now!"

"Meself!" snapped Brogeen.

"Why won't you be at the wedding?" asked the other sternly.

"Because I'll be on my way to where I'm most needed," replied Brogeen.

"You're needed here!" the King reminded him.

"I was only trying to help!" said Brogeen crossly. "Isn't it shocking always to be misunderstood!"

"Can my advice be of assistance?" asked a

voice, and there was the Chief Harper.

He had come back because he couldn't bear to be out of an argument.

"We need advice badly!" said the King. "Here's the trouble!"

The harper listened, his head bent.

"And now," concluded the King. "Brogeen wants to go off. Wouldn't you expect more reason from him?"

"He's right, your Majesty! He's right!"

"Right!" exclaimed the King, "Brogeen's always running off. And what good does he do?"

The harper folded his arms.

"Where his shoes are seen, no one is again satisfied with bad work. Just as those who hear our music never care for any other. There should be more of us going the roads of the world. We can always come back!"

"You're a great talker and that's the truth!" muttered the King. "Here's the Queen! Not a word to her, Brogeen! Do as you suggested. Gather up all the shoes you can find. We'll have another talk later on. Now I'm so flummoxed I can't think!"

"Why are you gossiping here, when the whole Court is waiting for dinner?" asked the Queen. "I'm hungry! If I weren't the most patient person in the Fort I'd have ordered dinner to be served without waiting for King or harper. There's my crown! You had it all the time!"

"Don't forget the shoes!" hissed the King over his shoulder.

"I won't, your Majesty!" promised Brogeen, with a low bow.

3

Shoes!

rogeen soon had all the young leprechauns and cluricauns collecting shoes. They packed them in sacks of gossamer, so light the wind carried them over rocks and trees, a cluricaun seated on each sack. Brogeen longed to go with them but he determined to stay in the Fort until the last shoe was packed.

"I don't trust them mischievous cluricauns," he thought. "They're always up to tricks. Someone must stay and who can I trust except meself!"

He strutted around proudly. He had never felt so important in his life.

The whole of Sheen was in an uproar. The Keeper of the Door dared not leave it open and he grew tired of opening and shutting, opening and shutting.

"This entrance is for visitors!" he declared. "I'll not have me clean doorstep dirtied with a parcel of bagmen! Find other ways! Not another shoe will go past me!"

"Of all the impudence!" grumbled Brogeen, when he heard this. "Go by holes and crevices in and out among the rocks. Off with you! You'll need to be home before dawn!"

He had cleared every press. Still there weren't enough shoes.

"I'll be disgraced when it gets round that I wouldn't send shoes to me own friends!" grumbled the King. "The way you've bragged, Brogeen, I thought there'd be enough shoes for everyone in the country!"

"Bragged!" exclaimed Brogeen indignantly. "Me bragged!"

"Then find more shoes!" ordered the King, stretching himself comfortably.

Brogeen put his head on one side and grinned.

"What about asking the Queen, your Majesty?"

The King looked at him scornfully.

"You would think of that. Ask her yourself!"

"I will so!" declared Brogeen, giving himself a shake.

"Bragger!" scoffed the King.

Brogeen was furious!

"Bragger!" he thought. "I'll show him. Bragger indeed!"

The leprechaun strutted up the marble steps, along a corridor with pictures on the walls, pictures which were changing all the time, even while he looked at them.

"Isn't it queer I never noticed them goings-on before!" wondered Brogeen. "It's a real good picture gallery! I should come here oftener!"

The Queen wasn't in her sun parlour though several of her maids-in-waiting were, practising a new dance for the wedding.

"Where's her Majesty?" asked Brogeen.

"The Queen is in the sulks upstairs. She won't see anyone. Come and dance with us!"

Brogeen was tempted. But he couldn't forget that the King had called him "Bragger!"

"No time!" he answered. "I've business with the Queen!"

They made a ring round him so that he couldn't go up the winding stairs to the Queen's tower. He leaped over their heads and there he was grinning down at them.

"I'll talk to you lassyoes on me way back," he said.

The stairs went up and round, up and round until he was dizzy. At last he came to a door at the top. He heard a voice singing—

> "I am so sad,
>   I could almost cry,
> When I see a blue butterfly
>   Drifting low, drifting high.
>
> "When raindrops fall
>   In a silver shower,
> Seeking the earth
>   Beneath my tower:
>
> "When birds fly south
>   In a long dark V,
> Over the endless,
>   Wind-tossed sea,
>
> "I feel so sad
>   I must dance or ride,
> Away on the wind,
>   Away on the tide."

"Oh dear!" sighed the Queen. "I wish—I wish I knew what to wish!"

"Isn't this shocking!" exclaimed Brogeen. "I wish I'd stayed below and minded me business!"

He could slide the whole way down. But the

maids would know he hadn't ventured to knock at the door.

"Yet the Queen wouldn't want anyone to be listening and she in such a state. 'Twasn't listening! How could I help hearing? I'd best be off and not say a word!" decided Brogeen.

The maids' voices rose. They were singing and laughing as they danced. The leprechaun longed to be with them, yet he couldn't leave the Queen when she was in trouble.

He tapped softly on the door.

"Mebbe she won't hear," he thought hopefully. "Then I can go away in peace and no harm done!"

"Come in, Brogeen!"

"Can you beat that!" he muttered, swinging open the door, and was inside before he had time to change his mind.

The Queen was leaning from a window in the tower, her elbows on the sill, her crown tossed upside down upon a cushion.

The tower was so high it pierced the clouds. At sunrise and sunset it seemed made of gold. In the night it gleamed silver and in the daytime it was a tall slender rock. Sweet-smelling flowers grew wherever they could find root-hold and not a bird passed without singing. Butterflies rested there on their sea journeys. Rain fell more gently and the wind parted on reaching the Queen's tower.

Many had seen it without knowing what they saw, even when the Queen's wondering eyes looked down at them.

Now she glanced over her shoulder.

"Oh, Brogeen! What a solemn face! Are you sad too?"

The leprechaun considered.

"Not sad, your Majesty. A bit concerned, you might say worried, not sad. What's troubling yourself?"

She swung round.

"Nothing, Brogeen! Nothing! I just thought I'd try being sad for a change, only I don't know what to be sad about. Do you remember any sad songs? I can't!"

"If 'tis sadness you want, let the Chief Harper play the Song of Sorrow as he played it the night Batt Kelly came to Sheen!"

Now the Queen did look sad.

"I'm ashamed, Brogeen! We're so happy here. I forget the world on the other side. You've been there. Is it very unhappy?"

"There's sadness yonder!" answered the leprechaun. "Not all the time and not for everyone. They could do with more happiness."

"I'll talk to the Chief Harper. He'll know what to do about it," decided the Queen.

She turned to the window.

"Look, Brogeen! Why are those silly young cluricauns trying to fly with those big clumsy sacks? They're no good at flying!"

"They're doing their best!" protested the leprechaun.

He drew a deep breath.

"They're taking shoes to the Knockmealdown mountains. The ones beyond, nearly out of sight, are making for the Mitchelstown Caves."

"Shoes!" exclaimed the Queen. "Shoes to the Knockmealdown mountains! How very strange!"

She laughed so much she nearly fell from the window. Brogeen pulled her back.

"'Tisn't that funny!" he snapped. "If 'twasn't for the shoes the poor lads are carrying there'd be a mighty small company to wish luck to Princess and her Merman!"

"I don't understand!" said the Queen.

She picked up her crown, put it on and became very dignified.

"I'll explain!" Brogeen told her.

She listened so earnestly Brogeen forgot to be nervous. When he had finished he looked at her anxiously.

"Mebbe I've no right to be troubling your Majesty," he muttered.

"You are quite right!" she declared. "Listen, Brogeen! I haven't liked to say it before, but you make more shoes for me than I can ever wear. They're so lovely, I just put them away. Lately I haven't known what to do, for every hole and corner is packed. Would you mind very much if we sent them to the Little People of The Windy Gap? I noticed last time they came what shabby shoes they were wearing, and they weren't the only ones!"

"If you let me take those, we'll be made up and I can start off on me travels," said the leprechaun.

"You're going away again?" asked the Queen.

Brogeen explained.

"I shall miss you," she said, really sorrowfully. "Before I feel too sad, call up the girls and I'll start them sorting out the shoes. But those you made for special occasions are so beautiful I don't know how I'll part with them!"

Brogeen ran the whole way down without stopping once. At the bottom the maids-in-waiting ran round him, holding a chain of flowers.

"The Queen wants you upstairs," he told them. "You're to turn out all the shoes that aren't really needed. Pack them up to be taken to the Macgillycuddy Reeks, the Knocknaskagh mountains and keep out a few for The Windy Gap."

The maids dropped the chain of flowers. "Give away the Queen's shoes!" they cried in horror.

"And your own too," added the leprechaun, grinning at them.

"Why can't they make their own shoes?" asked one maid. "When did you make a shoe?" asked Brogeen. "'Tis us leprechauns make the shoes and those poor benighted creatures haven't a leprechaun near them!"

"How strange!" cried the maids in amazement.

"We'll alter all that!" bragged Brogeen. "Only it takes time. Go up now and pack hard. Pull out all the shoes you can find and pack! pack! pack! Or there'll be no dancers at the wedding!"

They swept up the stairs, laughing and throwing the flower chain from hand to hand. The leprechaun, scurrying down the corridor, bumped into a cluricaun dragging a sack of shoes as big as himself.

The cluricaun dropped the sack and the shoes clattered over the marble floor.

Brogeen picked up a green boot with long ribbons.

"I made that for the Queen to wear the night we rode to the Rath of the Horned Women over by Golasparra. This satin shoe was for the dance the old unicorn gave in the Glen of the Larks. That was a wonderful night!"

The cluricaun listened in amazement.

"You never made a pair of shoes for me!" he grumbled.

His mischievous face grew sulky.

"Why didn't you let me learn to make shoes?" he asked. "Then I'd have been a leprechaun. I'd make myself a new pair of shoes every day and I'd let the rest go barefoot."

"There's your answer!" said Brogeen scornfully. "Fill that sack again and be off, or you'll not dance at the wedding!"

"I can't dance!" wailed the young fellow.

Brogeen stooped and picked up a pair of buckled shoes.

"Wear these and you'll dance till you're dizzy," he said. "Don't waste a moment or you'll have the Merman from the Cliffs of

Moher chasing you out to sea!"

He trotted on feeling very proud and important. He passed the Chief Harper who was looking out of the big door.

"The sky is cloudy but 'twill clear," he said. "When are you going, Brogeen?"

"I'm on me way!" replied the leprechaun, without thinking what he was saying.

"Where are your tools? How can you face the world outside without the tools of your trade?"

Brogeen looked foolish. He was ashamed to say that he hadn't really thought about when he would be going.

"I clean forgot. I was so puffed up giving out advice to a young cluricaun, that I was going empty-handed."

He went for his bag.

4

On the Road

rogeen hadn't meant to leave the Fort so quickly. He hadn't said good-bye. But the Keeper of the Door was always in a hurry and the leprechaun heard the slam which told him he was shut out.

In his hand were three shining silver coins the cross old Keeper had thrust at him as he marched through.

"I suppose we'll be seeing you when they're spent!" the Keeper muttered crossly.

"Mebbe and mebbe not!" retorted the leprechaun.

He kicked a stone. The sun was coming up over Slieve Mish. A lark soared suddenly into the golden air. A white hare darted across the path, stopped, turned and raced downhill.

"I'll not go back in a hurry!" decided Brogeen. "Where will I go first, up hill or down?"

Of course he went down.

"I'll take the left, then I'll take the right. I'll keep on going to the left and the right till I can't go any further. Then I'll stop. By that time I'll surely be in one of those places where they're always in want of shoes."

He caught up with a man leading a donkey which drew a cart loaded with black turf. The man had a slean on his shoulder and walked from side to side. The donkey went with him and they were so slow Brogeen grew impatient.

He dodged the cart, the donkey and the man and arrived safely in front of them.

"Grand day, mister!" he said.

"Grand enough for them that hasn't to work for a living!" complained the man. "I suppose you're with the tinkers I seen up along. Let me tell you, there's no love for tinkers in these parts!"

"I'm not a tinker!" protested Brogeen.

"Well, your mammy and your daddy are, so 'tis all one. Run along now and don't be annoying me. I've enough on me mind!"

The leprechaun hurried on.

"Impidence!" he said out loud when he was sure the man couldn't hear him. "Tinker! Me—

the best leprechaun in Ireland! Why did I leave Sheen? I was appreciated there!"

The road came to a village and Brogeen, peeping in at the windows, saw women blowing up the smouldering turf with bellows, stirring blackened saucepans, filling teapots from steaming kettles hanging from chains over the hearth. He heard them calling—"Will you get up? You'll be late for the school!"

"I'd like a bellows!" thought Brogeen. "I could have great fun with a bellows!"

An old woman stood at her gate holding a bucket.

"Hallo, young lad!" she said. "You're a stranger in these parts!"

"Strange enough!" agreed Brogeen.

"Would you fill the bucket for me at the spring yonder? I haven't the strength to bring it meself and I don't like pump water."

Brogeen took the bucket.

"Half fill it," she told him. "You're only a wheeshy bit of a gorseen. You wouldn't be able for a bucket full!"

Indeed he found half a bucket of water as much as he could manage.

"Me son can carry a full bucket in each hand and never spill a drop," the old woman told him proudly. "He's away over the sea. Here's a cut of barmbrack for the help."

Brogeen ate the barmbrack as he marched along in the sunshine. The light, cakey bread was fresh and sweet, though there weren't any raisins or sultanas or peel in it, only a few currants and a pinch of spice.

As the sun grew hotter, Brogeen began to walk slowly. He heard a bell ringing and the children on the road started to run. Some were pulling on their coats, some ate cuts of bread and butter.

A boy tossed a ball before him and he was the last of the children, for the ball went over a wall into a field and he followed it. But for Brogeen that ball would be there to this day, for it rolled under a bush.

"I'll be late!" lamented the boy. "Me new ball! I'll be late! Me new ball!"

"There it is—under the bush—the withered thorn bush! Right under yer nose, ye eejit!" called Brogeen.

He flung a stone. It struck the ball which turned over and lay at the boy's feet.

He picked it up, scrambled back to the road and ran on.

"Thanks!" he called over his shoulder. "Welcome!" replied Brogeen.

The road was empty. The children were in

school, the men in the fields, the women in the houses.

" 'Tis a lonesome road!" grumbled the leprechaun. "I'd like to be on the way to a fair. I like fairs!"

Instead of walking on the roadway Brogeen trotted on top of the low wall. It was quite wide enough for his small feet and he could see further. The road ran beside a river. On the far bank were trees and the leprechaun was thinking how much quicker it would be if he had a boat and could float down the river, when something tapped him on the head.

"Who did that?" he cried indignantly.

The road was deserted. He seemed to be alone.

"Hi, Brogeen!" called a voice. "Goodbye, Brogeen"

He looked up. Sitting on an empty sack which floated in the air like a balloon were two of the cluricauns who had been taking the shoes over the country. They grinned and waved their hands.

"How dare you touch me!" cried the leprechaun. "Wait till I lay me hands on you!"

The bigger of the two looked anxious. The other wriggled with delight.

"You can't catch us!" he squeaked. "You can't

catch us!"

"I'll see about that !" muttered Brogeen.

He gave a jump, so high his fingers touched the sack, when a sharp gust of wind tossed sack and cluricauns out of his reach and away over the trees. As Brogeen dropped to the ground the sack sailed out of sight.

"The young limbs!" growled Brogeen.

He had fallen lightly, though his clothes were dusty and his precious bag scraped at one corner. But he couldn't help laughing when he remembered the cluricauns.

"All the same, they should show respect!" he thought severely.

When the sun was overhead Brogeen found a cool spot under a willow. He had brought a packet of food with him and when he dipped his cup into the water he had a drink of golden wine that made him sleepy. He curled up on a cushion of moss and gazed through the dancing leaves at the sky.

"When I've gone far enough I'll find a snug corner and build a little house, the kind I've always wanted."

He didn't know he had been asleep until music and a rushing sound, as if all the swallows in the neighbourhood were overhead, roused him.

He had slept so long, the sun had left the sky. The night was fine but clouds were streaming along, so low they almost touched the treetops.

Were they clouds?

Brogeen jumped to his feet and ran to the highest part of the river bank.

"They're not clouds! They're visitors from the Knockmealdown mountains and they'll be first at the Fort for the wedding. There'll be dancing and singing and feasting, and I'll not be there. Yet 'tis through me they can go and not be shamed!"

He stood on tiptoe, straining to see the groups who, flying, leaping, carried by the wind, were journeying to Slieve Mish.

"I could go aloft and join them," he thought. "Wasn't I foolish not to wait for the wedding? Haven't I as much right as anyone to be there? 'Twas the Chief Harper had me so confused, I was out of the Fort before I knew what I was doing!"

Yet he didn't take the jump that would start him on the way back.

"I've something more important than weddings to attend to!" decided Brogeen. "Haven't I me work to do? Let them go on with their fun and merrymaking. I've to take me place in this queer strange world."

The next day the roads were crowded. Brogeen had no need to walk, or jump, or fly. He took a lift on a sidecar, and no one saw him, only the horse went at a gallop, instead of a trot. He swung on a lorry and set the boys and girls packed in it singing and laughing, yet not a soul knew he was there.

So he came to the Puck Fair at Kilorglin.

This was the first day, the day of the gathering. As Brogeen came into the little town, climbing the hill above the river, the big goat, King of the Fair, was being lifted to his throne in the centre of the crowded square. There was no room anywhere else, so up went the leprechaun and settled himself beside the Goat King.

"Go along out of that!" said the goat. "This is my throne! If ye stay a minute longer, I'll puck ye off with me two good horns!"

"Puck away!" retorted Brogeen cheerfully. "I'll not interfere with you if you don't interfere with me. I'm all the way from Slieve Mish and I'm tired of the lonely roads. This is a grand place! 'Twas worth giving up the wedding of the Princess to the Merman."

"What brings you on the roads?" asked the goat. "Did they throw you out of your Fort?

You're a leprechaun, aren't ye? Is the trouble that you can't make shoes?"

Brogeen laughed, so did the goat. The people could see the goat but they couldn't see the leprechaun.

"Look at the King Goat enjoying himself!" they said. "He's the best we've had in years!"

"Why wouldn't he be enjoying himself?" asked the leader of the band. "Look at the grand food he's eating and we killing ourselves playing music in his honour!"

A basket, piled with tiny carrots, small onions, sprigs of thyme and sage, and golden turnips, like oranges, stood before the goat.

"Help yerself!" he told Brogeen. "There'll be plenty more! They feed a chap well at the Fair!"

"Why wouldn't they?" cried the leprechaun. "Aren't you the King? I wonder now, did you ever hear of a nice handy place where a lad like meself could set up in trade? I've a great wish for a little house, with friendly neighhours, not too far from a stream, and a road; a place where there's sunshine and not too much wind."

The goat munched thoughtfully.

"I did!" he said at last. "What's more I've seen it! Over that way, where the sun comes in the morning there's a mighty fine river. Keep on till you come to the Bridge of the Seven Arches. Cross over and keep going to the third crossroads. Up along, on the right, at the foot of the mountain, is a boreen. There's a stream on one side and a shocking lot of birds live there. Where it joins the road there's a blackthorn and a whitethorn the only proper place I know for a leprechaun that's setting up on his own."

Brogeen was excited.

"Would it be far from the Knockmealdown mountains and the Knocknaskagh mountains?"

"Far enough, but not too far!"

"I'm on me way!" said Brogeen.

"What's the hurry?" asked the goat. "Stay for the scattering. You and me could be great friends."

"I'll be seeing you!" called Brogeen. "You know the address!"

He gave a leap that took him across the nearest roof and kept on leaping till he was out of the town. He used the road then, because he liked walking, when he hadn't too much of it and he wanted to think of all he'd do when he came to the boreen with the blackthorn and the whitethorn beyond the Bridge of the Seven Arches.

5

Wanted—a House

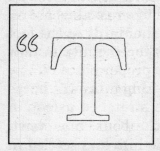ime I found a house!" said Brogeen.

"The shoes are worn off me feet!" he grumbled.

"I need a rest. I was never one for keeping on and keeping on," he told a timid field-mouse, who peeped at him from behind a withered barley stalk. "And I'm tired of the hard, long roads!"

The mouse crept away, hiding his tiny body but forgetting his tail, so that Brogeen could easily have followed him.

"Such foolishness!" he exclaimed, laughing so loudly the startled mouse gave a sudden leap and was gone.

"That one has a home!" sighed the leprechaun. "Wirra! Wirra! I'm a poor homeless creature! Why did I leave the Fort?"

"Will I never come to that Bridge of the

Seven Arches?" he asked, as he crossed a wide river.

He reached the other side and looked back.

"One, two, three, four, five, six, seven!" he counted. "Seven arches! I'm as good as there! The third crossroads! On the right! At the foot of the mountain! There's the mountain, now for the crossroads!"

A haycart drawn by a big brown horse jogged along, with a man stretched asleep in front, the reins twisted about his wrist. Brogeen jumped up beside him and settled in among the soft, springy hay to enjoy the rest of the journey.

The swaying of the cart, the steady tramp of the horse's hooves upon the road, made the leprechaun pleasantly sleepy. The splashing of water among rocks made him open one eye. He opened two.

"I'm there!" he cried. "A whitethorn and a blackthorn, a boreen by a stream— I'm home!"

"Wha—a?" asked the driver, but his eyes remained closed.

"Safe home and thanks for the ride!" said Brogeen, leaping to the road.

The boreen was sheltered by a row of bushes. It ended opposite a huge beech on the other side of the stream. The curved roots rose

out of the ground and the leaves fell in a
golden shower, piling up, toppling into the
stream and drifting away.

"If 'tis a, house you're wanting, why don't
you build one?" asked a voice.

Brogeen swung round. A blackbird, perched
on the stump of a fallen tree, was watching
him with its bright, friendly eye.

"I'm not a bird!" retorted the leprechaun.
"And I'm not asking advice about nests."

"No offence!" said the bird cheerfully,
rattling its yellow beak.

Brogeen was disgusted with his own bad
manners.

"Sorry!" he muttered. "I'm a bit strange and
tired, and I've never built a house in me life.
I'm a shoemaker by trade."

"A shoemaker! Then you're Brogeen the
leprechaun! We were told you were coming.
Hi, neighbours! Here's Brogeen come to live in
the boreen!"

There was a flurry of wings. The air was
filled with birds. Mice, beetles, a water rat, a
couple of rabbits and even a squirrel came
hurrying along.

"Welcome!" they cried. "Start the house!
We'll help!"

"Welcome, Brogeen, to our boreen.
'Tis the pleasantest boreen ever
    was seen.
You'll find berries and seed pods,
Nuts from the hazel bush
For breakfast and dinner.
For building there's rocks
And thick, well-dried sods.
There's grass and there's rushes,
There's twigs and big leaves
For roofing and eaves.
We'll help build a house
Bird, beetle and mouse,
So our new neighbour, Brogeen,
Can live down our boreen."

The wind swept down the mountain. The bushes quivered and the beech leaves fell faster.

"The rain's coming! It's here!" warned the blackbird. "Fly for shelter!"

Down came the rain. The birds scattered. Mice, beetles, scurried in under the bushes. Brogeen stood alone.

From the far side of the stream the blackbird called.

"Jump, Brogeen! You'll be safe here!"

The rain was trickling inside his jacket, his

cap was soaked, his feet growing wetter and wetter. He went back a little way, ran, leaped into the air and there he was in the dry, safe shelter of the beech.

"If I were you," said the blackbird, "I'd snuggle in under this root. It's draughty but there's dry leaves in plenty and here's a heap of blackberries we gathered in case you were hungry."

A whirl of wings and Brogeen was indeed alone.

Wind and rain swept past the beech but Brogeen, tucked up on a couch of leaves, ate the sweet, juicy blackberries contentedly. As he finished the last, he heard thunder rolling across the mountain. Yawning, he put his head down on his bag and fell asleep.

Chucklings, whisperings, thumpings were all round him but the leprechaun wouldn't open his eyes until he heard—

"Brogeen! Are you awake?"

He sat up. His friends of the night before were gathered about him, looking very proud of themselves.

"'Pon me word!" exclaimed Brogeen. "You've built the house!"

With the root for roof, it had been walled in on each side with sheets of bark. A hole had been left to come in and go out. Two logs, one big, for a table, one small, for a seat, had been rolled in. A pile of nuts lay on the table with a stone for cracking them.

"You're real neighbours," muttered Brogeen.

"Any time you want help, give a call," the blackbird told him. "We must be going!"

When they were gone, Brogeen rolled his seat to the door-way, cracked a handful of nuts and thought of the wonderful time in front of him.

"I'll make a door and put up me name. I'll carve a chest to keep me tools in. I'll build a fireplace for the winter. I'll send out word I'm ready to start shoemaking. I'll go visiting. I'll hear the news. Isn't it a good thing there's so much time in the world!"

6

The Stepping Stones

 rogeen made a door to his house that would swing right back. Over the top he carved his name.

BROGEEN
Shoemaker

He had a snug bed of dried leaves in the corner and, every time one of the neighbours looked in, there was something fresh to report.

"He's made a creepy and the three legs look as if they could walk up to you!"

"Would you believe it—Brogeen's making a fireplace!"

That brought everyone who lived in the boreen.

"Fire's a desperate thing to bring into your home!" chattered the squirrel. "I know the wren won't like it."

"Look!" said the leprechaun. "There's clay all round. The more fire I have, the harder the clay will grow. It might turn a lovely red. But the smoke will go out through that hole and be carried away by the wind. And you can tell the wren to mind his own business."

"I wouldn't do that! I wouldn't dream of doing that!" chattered the squirrel. "I'm glad you explained. I've more nuts than I need. I'll bring you some tonight!"

"Thank you kindly!" said the leprechaun. "And I didn't mean what I said about the wren. He's a decent little neighbour!"

The squirrel forgot the nuts. Brogeen didn't mind. He could gather all he wanted. Next he set to work on a table. He was proud of that table. When it was finished he gave a party. Most of the visitors sat under the table. The rest perched on top. Brogeen sat at the head on his creepy.

It was the first real party held in the boreen and the neighbours talked of it for days after.

When Brogeen announced that he would make a chest to keep his tools and treasures safe, even the blackbird, his oldest friend, looked serious.

"There's sense in a table!" he declared.

"There's not a haporth of mischief in a creepy. But whoever heard of a chest?"

"Don't be foolish!" snapped the leprechaun. "Sure a chest is only a wooden hole with a top to it!"

The blackbird brightened up. He polished his yellow beak on a branch of the beech.

"You've something there!" he said. "A hole with a lid! That's good! I'll tell the others. We were a bit worried. We thought you might be getting past yourself. But a hole with a lid to it—sure there's no harm in that!"

He went off chuckling.

When the leprechaun made his first pair of shoes, he put them on the table and invited the neighbours to look. They stood back and gazed in wonder.

Brogeen grew impatient at their silence.

"What do you think of them?" he demanded. "Speak up!"

They stared at the wren, the wisest of them all.

"Brogeen!" chirped the little bird. "We liked you from the first moment you came to the boreen. Now we're proud of you!"

The wren flew off at once, for he never had any time to waste. The leprechaun was so confused he didn't notice.

"Thanks!" he muttered. "You're very kind!"

"Not at all!" twittered the blackbird. "You're very welcome."

Brogeen was almost as conceited about his home as he was about his shoemaking. And now he had started work he was really happy.

Besides, he could go to the town at the other side of the Bridge of the Seven Arches as often as he wished. There was a market every Saturday and a fair once a month. If he felt shy he need not be seen. If he wanted to be friendly he could be a little old man. When he felt mischievous he could run and jump and play tricks like any of the boys on the road.

Every morning Brogeen went down the boreen and looked into the blackthorn bush. He would find a piece of leather, or velvet, or maybe a tiny piece of satin stuck in a forsaken nest. Then he set to work and made a pair of shoes or boots which he would hide in the whitethorn bush. Next time he looked they'd be gone but there was always a coin left in the nest, mostly silver but sometimes gold.

When Brogeen first came to live by the stream he had to leap across. He was a grand jumper so he didn't mind that. But one day, as he sprang over, the green rush basket on his arm—for he had been down to the fair to buy provisions—a bag of sugar fell into the water and he couldn't save a grain. Another evening, a jam sponge Brogeen had bought for tea went the same way. He fished it out as quickly as he could, yet it was sodden and though the little shoemaker dried it in front of the fire, it didn't taste the least bit like sponge cake.

"There's nothing for it but a bridge!" said Brogeen.

He gathered rocks and dropped them in the stream. They were washed away. He dragged branches from the beech and tried to lay them from bank to bank. But the leprechaun couldn't find any fallen ones long enough and, if he had, he wouldn't have had the strength to lift them.

He could have sent a message for help to the dwellers in the Knockmealdown mountains, or those in the Knocknaskagh, but he was too independent.

One night, as Brogeen lay stretched comfortably on his bed of dried leaves, a storm of wind and rain shook the world outside. When morning came and he poked out his head, the little shoemaker saw that three large flat stones had been washed down the stream opposite his door. They made as fine a bridge as any leprechaun could wish for.

If the stepping stones were good for Brogeen, they were just as good for others. One moonlight night he was eating supper by his fire and thinking what a lucky fellow he was, when he heard a knock on the door.

"Come along in!" said Brogeen.

Nothing happened.

"'Twas just a twig tapping!" he thought.

The knock came again.

"Lift the latch and in with ye!" snapped Brogeen.

The door stayed shut but the knock sounded a third time.

"Now wouldn't you think I'd the right to be left in peace by me own fire an' I after working hard all day!" grumbled the little shoemaker, as he got up from his stool and flung the door open.

Outside sat a phouka, shaggy and wild-looking. Brogeen wasn't the least bit frightened. Wasn't he in his own house?

"What brings you here at this hour of night?" he demanded. "Haven't I a right to my rest?"

The phouka held out one hoof and made a gentle neighing noise.

"I've no use for strange talk!" declared the leprechaun. "Shoemaking's me trade!"

The phouka looked pleadingly at Brogeen, who wasn't nearly as cross as he pretended to be.

"'Tis dancing shoes I make, or it might be riding boots," he explained. "A creature like yerself would be wanting horse's shoes. 'Tis a blacksmith you should be seeking."

The phouka neighed so sorrowfully that Brogeen stood back from the door.

"Come along in and rest yourself! I might be able to think where you should be making for."

The phouka followed him in and they sat together in front of the fire.

Brogeen tried not to but he couldn't help looking at the phouka's hoofs. They were quite worn down and it wouldn't take so clever a shoemaker as the leprechaun to know the poor thing would be hurt every time he stepped on a stone.

"Something must be done!" muttered Brogeen.

The phouka neighed. This time Brogeen did understand.

"You're very kind," was what the phouka said, and he settled himself more comfortably.

The creature's hoofs were so small, Brogeen thought he might manage. He brought out two strips of silver and two of gold and laid them on the last made of white wood. Then he hammered and hammered until four tiny horseshoes rested side by side.

"Now we'll fit them!" said Brogeen.

He put them to the phouka's hoofs and they stuck as if they had grown there.

The phouka stood up and shook himself.

"Open the door!" he neighed.

Brogeen opened the door.

"Giving orders!" he thought indignantly. "Isn't it me own house?"

The phouka stepped through. He tossed his mane and tail, and stamped as if to test his new shoes. Then away with him, over the stepping stones and down the boreen out of sight.

"Gold and silver shoes, and not a word of thanks from him!" exclaimed Brogeen. "This ignorant, uncultivated creature!"

He went in and slammed the door.

Two nights later—it was a cold, bitter night, with the wind howling and moaning through the beech—Brogeen was snug and warm by his fire of tiny logs. He had a pot of tea and a hot griddle cake thickly buttered. On his feet were a pair of soft red felt slippers, and he propped them up on a stool so that he could admire them.

"There's nothing to beat the first sup of tea on a wild night after a hard day's work!" said Brogeen.

A loud rap sounded on the door.

"'Tis the wind!" declared Brogeen. "If I'm not the lucky one to be in the warm, safe and taking me ease!"

"Bang! Bang! Bang!" came from the other side of the door.

"Will you come in!" cried the leprechaun. "Come in and bad scran to you, whoever you are!"

The door opened and in crept an old bent woman. The tatters of her shawl dripped, her boots were broken, and Brogeen could see that her feet were cut by the rocky mountain paths.

"Take a seat by the fire, ma'am!" he said, lifting his feet from the stool. "I'll pour you a sup of the best tea you'll drink in a month of Sundays!"

"Thank ye kindly, sir!" whispered the old woman.

She held her thin hands to the blaze and looked about her. Brogeen put a cup of tea on the hearth and a plate of hot griddle cake beside it.

"You've a real grand little home," she said, speaking so softly Brogeen wouldn't have

heard a word, only his ears were as sharp as
his awl.

"'Tisn't many has a home like mine!" he
boasted. "That's sure enough."

The old woman sipped the tea and ate the
cake slowly, tasting every morsel.

"Me poor feet," she sighed. "Going the roads
is terrible hard on the boots and I haven't had
a new pair since dear knows when!"

"'Tis a hard life surely," agreed the
leprechaun sorrowfully.

"Musha!" she said. "What ails me? Haven't I
had a grand cup of tay with two spoonfuls of
sugar and a cut of hot, buttered griddle cake!
What right have I to complain? Thank you
kindly, sir, I must be on me way."

She stood up. Brogeen could see the muddy
water squelching from her broken boots.

"Sit down!" he ordered sternly. "You'll not
set foot from this house till you have boots that
will keep you dry and sound. Sit yourself
down, ma'am!"

The old woman sat down again and blinked
happily at the fire.

From the polished wooden chest. Brogeen
brought out a piece of black leather. He
smoothed it, cut out a pair of boots, then
tapped in the nails so quickly, pushed the

thread in and out at such a rate, the old woman was still dreaming when the leprechaun held out to her the boots he had made.

"Put them on, ma'am!" he said. "And let me tell you that's the quickest I've ever worked!"

She pulled off her old boots, thrust her feet into the new ones and stood up.

"I haven't a gold piece to give you, Mister Shoemaker. But I wish you the best of luck and a friend when you need one most!"

She was out through the door while Brogeen was offering her a shakedown for the night.

The next day, and the day after, the leprechaun was so hard at work he didn't stir from the house. On the third morning, with a little pair of riding boots under his arm, he crossed over by the stepping stones and trotted down the boreen.

He had almost reached the thornbushes when he heard Tap! Tap! Tap! Another shoemaker must be at work!

Laying the boots carefully on the grass, Brogeen peeped out behind the blackthorn. A tall, red-haired lad who lived beyond the crossroads was hammering a boot with a stone from the roadway. His little sister sat perched on the bank, her feet dangling, and she wore only one boot.

Brogeen couldn't bear to see a job badly done. He stepped out on the road.

"You young eejit!" he cried. "Hand over the boot! That's no way at all to be hammering and banging!"

He snatched the boot and frowned at it.

"There's a nail sticking up inside," explained the little girl. "It's digging such a hole in me foot I can't walk."

Brogeen had his hammer stuck in his belt. He pulled it out. The boy and girl stared in amazement.

"Did you see the gold head to his hammer, Jim?" whispered the girl.

"I did indeed, Judy, and the gold buckle on his apron," the boy whispered back. "Don't let on!"

Brogeen gave the boot one tap with his hammer.

"That's fixed!" he said. "You'll have no more trouble with that!"

"You're awful good!" said Judy, hopping down to take her boot. "I've always wanted to meet a leprechaun!"

Brogeen was so startled he dropped the boot on the road, darted off and didn't stop running until he was safely indoors.

"Wasn't I the foolish fellow!" he exclaimed. "Why did I let meself be seen, working, by strangers? They might have caught me and held me prisoner till I gave up me crock of gold! Isn't it time I learned sense!"

He forgot all about the riding boots he had left lying on the grass until he found them there the following morning. They were soaked with dew and he had to take them home to be dried and polished.

"A day wasted! And all because I couldn't keep meself to meself!" grumbled Brogeen.

He sat up half the night, cutting, stitching, hammering a pair of children's boots he hoped to sell at the fair.

Brogeen hadn't forgotten that part of his work was to show people how shoes should be made.

7

Brogeen at the Fair

rogeen had found out about the markets and fairs at the town beyond the river. The day of the first fair since he had come to the boreen, he woke early, sure that this would be the best fair he had ever seen.

Yawning and sleepy, for all his excitement, the little shoemaker was across the stepping stones, down the boreen and out on the road at the first glimmer of daylight.

He wasn't the only one on the road. There were horses and carts, lorries, donkeys, bicycles and people, men and women, and so many boys and girls, Brogeen was bewildered. He scrambled on the back of a cart and when a man, riding a horse, caught up, he sprang behind him so lightly, neither horse nor rider knew what had happened.

A great lorry came thundering along.

Horses, donkeys, carts, had to squeeze against the walls to make room. When it came level with the rider Brogeen gave a jump and landed just behind the driver's seat. So he was one of the earliest at the fair.

Brogeen hated crowds, yet he loved fairs. He trotted round, holding his basket in front of him, standing on tiptoe to look at the stalls and staring at the swings.

He stopped at the hobby horses and made up his mind to have a ride. But he hadn't sold the boots yet and he had no money.

Opposite the hobby horses he saw a boot shop.

"There's the place!" he thought. "'Tis packed with rubbish. The man will be thankful to see a bit of decent work!"

Brogeen went across, took the boots from his basket and was stepping into the shop when a young tinker came strolling through the fair. He was bare-foot and ragged, but he whistled as gaily as if he owned everything there. Like Brogeen, he stopped outside the boot shop.

Shoes and boots were hanging in bunches on each side of the door. Suddenly the young tinker reached out and snatched a pair of brown shoes.

The shopkeeper was just inside the door.

"Stop thief!" he roared, and darted out.

Off went the tinker lad and off went Brogeen! The leprechaun was too startled to know why he was running and then he was too frightened to stop and wish himself not to be seen.

Everyone they passed stared after him, heard the shout "Stop thief!" and joined the chase, shouting too.

The shopkeeper was puzzled. He had seen the young tinker stealing the shoes but he was sure Brogeen had not touched any of his goods. Yet there he was, racing away, a pair of boots dangling from his hands.

"Two thieves at one time!" he thought. "How can a man live? I'll murder them!"

The young tinker gave the leprechaun a push, dodged behind a cart and squeezed into the crowd around a fortune teller. Brogeen went on running and after him trailed his pursuers.

"We'll gaol the thieves!" cried a man carrying a big stick. "Stop thief!" shouted the others.

Brogeen was breathless. He could hardly see. He wanted to throw down the boots but his fingers wouldn't let go. Instead, he dropped his basket.

"I'll have one of them!" shouted the shopkeeper, wondering where the young tinker had gone. "I'll lodge him in gaol! I'll have his life!"

Brogeen stumbled. He couldn't run another step. A stone whizzed by.

A tall, redheaded boy was standing on the curb, his sister beside him. Both were eating hot apple cake.

"Jim! There's our little shoemaker!" cried the girl. "They're chasing him!"

"Leave the little chap alone!" shouted Jim, stepping out between the leprechaun and the crowd.

"You should be ashamed!" cried Judy.

They were pushed on one side, but Brogeen had gained.

"They helped! But I'll not last much longer," he thought in despair. "If only I had time to stand still and wish!"

Up a side street came a huge goat, leading a flock of sheep. He swung out between Brogeen and the angry mob, while the sheep spread across the road like waves of the sea.

The leprechaun was caught up by the great curving horns. There he sat, safe on the goat's back.

Out of the fair they raced, out of the town.

The goat slowed down and gently slid Brogeen to the ground.

"You brought me out the wrong side of the town!" complained the leprechaun. "I'm miles from me home. You should carry me there!"

Then he stared.

"You're no billygoat!" he exclaimed. "You're the phouka I made the shoes for!"

He stared again.

"I know you now! You're the King of Puck Fair! Isn't it great to see you here! Yet you're only a phouka after all!"

The phouka neighed and galloped away, leaving Brogeen gazing after him and looking very puzzled.

"Here's yer basket, Mister Shoemaker!" said a voice behind him.

Brogeen turned and there was the old Woman of the Roads, holding out his basket neatly packed with parcels.

"I did the bit of shopping for ye," she said.

And off she went, so quickly only a phouka could have overtaken her.

"I'm safe and I've me basket full, though I've still me boots to sell!" muttered Brogeen. "But where am I at all?"

A river flowed before him. As he watched it

grew narrower and narrower. Three stepping stones led to the far bank and there, among the roots of the beech tree, was his own snug home.

"If this don't beat all!" said Brogeen, as he stepped dryshod across the stream.

8

Peter the Pedlar

Brogeen was one of the best shoemakers in the whole country and he was indeed proud of his work. But he had his troubles.

One spring day Brogeen was feeling terribly discontented. The sun was shining and the black, bare branches of the bushes which grew along the stream were studded with tiny white flowers, so that when Brogeen first looked out he was delighted. But when he opened his door wide, a bitter wind swept down the mountain, the thorn blossoms shivered and Brogeen shut his door in a hurry.

"Cheating!" he exclaimed indignantly.

"The sun shining and the cold would cut the nose off your face! And me out of logs and turf! Wirra! Wirra! I wish 'twas hot summer. I'm tired of the cold and darkness, and the lonesomeness of winter!"

He pulled his cap over his ears, wrapped a thick red muffler round and round his neck, went out and slammed the door behind him quickly so that he wouldn't change his mind.

"Mebbe I was foolish to leave the Fort. I could have let the others go out into the world. The happiness I gave up! Wirra! Wirra!"

He had a sack under one arm for logs and his little axe under the other.

Running across the stepping stones, he didn't go down the boreen but turned the other way by the high rock where the stream fell down, up the mountain where the woodman had been felling trees. He hunched his shoulders against the cold and wished he were still in bed.

"Yet I wasn't too warm these last few days," he grumbled. "I should have more dried leaves under me and a new rush mat on top!"

He was happier when he reached the wood. The cutters had left thick chips in heaps and the sack was quickly filled without Brogeen having to do any chopping at all.

The trees sheltered him from the wind and now he felt the warmth of the sun. Sitting on his bulging sack, he folded his arms and gazed down on his own boreen, along the road, over the Bridge of the Seven Arches, right to the town.

"I left the Fort of me own free will," said Brogeen, talking to himself. "I wanted a little house of me own. I have one! I wanted to be on me lone and independent. So I am! Then why am I complaining!"

Smoke rose thinly from the chimneys, for the morning was still young.

"Where there's smoke there's fire and where there's fire at this hour of the day there'll be breakfasts," murmured Brogeen. "Wisha! I could do with a steaming hot dish of stirabout, or a cup of strong, sweet tea and a good slice of hot, buttered toast."

He was hungry but he didn't move, for now, on the road, he saw a green and red caravan, pulled by a fat, comfortable horse, who lifted each leg carefully and thoughtfully, without the least sign of hurry.

The caravan had a chimney and blue smoke from a wood fire streamed on the wind.

"There's luxury!" sighed Brogeen. "There's grandeur! Travelling the roads and eating and sleeping as you go! 'Tis the only way to see the world, the only way—for them that has the means!"

He stood up and started down hill, dragging the sack along the ground, for it was too heavy to lift. When he reached the stepping stones, he couldn't manage it at all. He half-emptied the sack, carried it over, tipped the chips into a sheltered corner, brought the other half and set to work to make up his fire.

It was nearly out. The great ash was crumbling into a smaller and smaller heap.

"I should have a turf-pile. Logs throw out a grand heat but they don't last. Make a turf fire and your troubles are finished."

With a hot cup of tea and a cut of soda bread spread with honey, Brogeen sat before his crackling fire.

Now he was warm and at ease but he was still discontented.

"Look at me," he complained. "I wanted to see the world. What have I done? I've been nowhere, seen nothing! I cut and hammer and sew—that's all! I haven't been visiting. I haven't even seen the ones who wear the shoes I make. If I had a caravan. But I haven't! If I had a donkey, or even a goat, but I haven't—I'd go off on my travels and see the world. Only I've nothing but my own two feet!"

He stretched his legs before him and shook

his head. Brogeen was only a little fellow. His legs were short and his feet tiny. Unless he could beg or borrow a lift it took him a whole day to go into town and back again, and the world was a big place. He knew that.

"'Tis the going and the coming that has me beat!" thought the leprechaun. "If I saved on the coming and kept going? That's the style, me lad! You'd be getting somewhere! I'd need a good, stout pair of shoes with thick soles to them. Whisha! Where'd I come across the leather for travelling shoes? Where would I now?"

While Brogeen stitched and hammered, he longed to be on his travels. He had some stew in the pot and he warmed that up for his dinner. Then, instead of going on with his work, he smartened himself and went in search of advice.

The little shoemaker didn't often go visiting. When he was half-way across the stepping stones, he stood still, wondering which of his new friends he should consult.

Timmy Bucko, another leprechaun, had come to live farther round the mountain—but he was a stay-at-home. There was the phouka, who could often be found by the quarry, but he was wild and unreliable. Jim

MacDonald and his sister Judy were a grand pair—only young and had never been away from these parts. He went through all his local friends and shook his head at each one of them.

"'Pon me word!" he declared. "I've as many friends as the next one but there isn't one of them has seen more of the world than their own corner. I'll just stray around and I might happen to meet with a great traveller. Here's hoping!"

He trotted down the boreen, between the stream and the bushes. The blackbird came darting up from behind a clump of primrose already in bloom, singing as if he were going for a holiday. He stopped suddenly when he saw Brogeen and settled down for a chat.

"Hallo! Hallo!" said the blackbird.

"Hallo yourself!" returned the leprechaun. "You put the heart across me, shooting out that bold way!"

"A grand day, a gorgeous day, a fine hardy day!" whistled the blackbird, flirting its tail. "Thanks be I've a snug, safe nest!"

"'Tis a hard, bitter day that's freezing me nose, me toes and me fingers!" growled Brogeen. "Have you ever been travelling?"

"Up and down!" sang the blackbird, dancing

as if he couldn't keep still. "Up and down, along the boreen, down the road, up the mountain. But when this lot of young ones are raised, me an' the missus have decided we'll look round a bit."

"That's not travelling!" shouted the leprechaun, so crossly the thrushes, the robins, the sparrows, even the wren who lived on the boreen, came popping out to discover what was the trouble.

"Is there one of you, just one, that's ever seen a bit of the world beyond the boreen, the road and the mountain?" demanded the leprechaun. "Answer me that now!"

The birds looked at one another, put their heads on one side, shook them and went back to their own affairs, for this was their busy season of the year. Only the wren remained.

"You're not thinking of shifting and you so well fixed?" asked the little bird anxiously. "You'll not find a pleasanter place to live than the boreen. Ah, sure, you wouldn't give up your lovely little house! We'd all be terrible sorry to lose such a good neighbour, so we could. The blackbird would be destroyed. He thinks the world of you!"

"I'm wanting to travel!" explained Brogeen. "If I could meet with another traveller, he might advise me the best way to start."

"Why not wait till the swallows come back?" suggested the wren. "Doesn't everyone know they're the greatest travellers there are? They should be here any day now!"

"Mebbe so," muttered Brogeen. "But they're too slow in coming to please me."

The wren fluttered his wings and vanished. Brogeen marched on. All along the boreen the birds were singing—

"I'm going to build a nest
In the bush I like the best.
In the big whitethorn with its
    blossoming cloud,
I'm going to build a nest.

"I've a nest already made,
There my blue eggs will be laid.
Where the pale flowers shine on the
    blackthorn bush,
I've a nest already made.

"I—I come from far away.
Sure, I only arrived today.
The loveliest thing is a thorn in flower!
It's that I'm striving to say.

"Tweet! Tweet! I'll build a nest!
Tirra la! I've made the best!
Tirra lu! I'll sing all day
In the thornbushes where I'll rest!"

Brogeen beat his hands together and
stamped to make his feet warm. Instead of
making sure the road was deserted, he came
jumping out of the boreen and nearly tripped
over a man sprawling on the bank.

"Oh! Oh! Oh!" cried Brogeen.

"Ow! Ow! Ow!" mimicked the man. "Ye're
the selfsame chap I've been waiting on."

The man was a pedlar. Brogeen had seen
him at the fair many a time. But they had
never spoken before.

"Why were you wanting me?" demanded
the leprechaun, stepping out of reach.

"No need to be frightened of Peter the
Pedlar," the man told him. "I'm an honest
tradesman like yerself. I never get up to
tricks. Wait now till I open me pack and ye'll
see something I've been saving till I met one
of your kind."

"Who told you about me?" asked Brogeen
suspiciously.

"Batt Kelly, the fiddler from Dunquin, to be
sure!"

The leprechaun smiled.

"I know Batt!" he said.

"So do I!" declared the pedlar. "A fine chap now he's changed. I asked him where he'd lost his bad temper and he laughed at me. Batt Kelly laughing! And his playing! He usen't to be too bad with the jigs and reels and a few marches. But now! I could listen to him till Tibb's Eve! I axed him had he been sleeping in a fairy fort!"

Peter stared at Brogeen. Brogeen looked at the ground.

"Did he tell you?" asked the leprechaun softly.

"He did not! Mebbe you could. But I'll ask no awkward questions. Sit here alongside me on the bank."

Brogeen was curious. He watched while the pedlar opened his pack, showing rolls of ribbon, papers of pins and needles, cards of buttons, tubes of toothpaste, cakes of pink scented soap. Peter lifted them out and arranged them neatly where the sun had dried the grass. At last he uncovered a piece of green leather, thick and soft, stroking it with his fingertips, he held it out so that it glimmered in the pale sunlight.

Brogeen put his fist to his mouth to prevent

himself from crying out. He had never seen such leather in his life. He could not keep his hands from it. He sprang forward, then, terrified at his daring, tried to leap back and went rolling on the road.

The pedlar stretched his long arm and set the little shoemaker on his feet.

"Listen now," he said. "We're both friends of Batt Kelly. Doesn't that make everything right between us? I'm not after yer crock of gold. I've a pocketful of good shillings and pennies that's more use to me. Now—me fine fella—d'ye want to trade with me?"

Brogeen sat down. He had to. His legs were trembling.

"Indeed I want to trade with you, Peter the Pedlar!" he said.

"I've never seen a lovelier bit of leather! 'Twill do grand for the pair of shoes I'll need to go on me travels!"

"Your travels!" exclaimed Peter. "I'm wanting ye to make a pair of boots for me, a pair of boots that will carry me over the roads without tiredness. Ye're the best shoemaker in Ireland and that's good enough for me!"

"Me make boots for the likes of you?" cried Brogeen. "Me! A leprechaun make boots for a pedlar!"

"Why not?" asked Peter.

" 'Tis this way," explained Brogeen. "We make for our own kind, and now and again for a child, to sell at a fair. That takes us all the time there is. But I'll make you an offer for the bit of leather. I've a notion for it!"

"Ye're nothing better than a gombeen man!" exclaimed Peter. "I'm disappointed in ye. I've stood up for the leprechauns against tinkers, balled singers and storytellers. I've given them a good name! In the time to come I'll keep me mouth shut. Ah well! There's a few cobblers in the country yet can make a pair of shoes!"

"You couldn't hand that lovely leather to an ordinary cobbler! You couldn't do it!" declared Brogeen.

"I'll be on me way," said Peter. "I'll most likely get rheumatiz in me bones, waiting here on a leprechaun that wouldn't do a poor travelling man a good turn. An' me thinking how grand I'd be looking on Easter Sunday morning. I'll let Batt Kelly know what I think of his friend the leprechaun. I can guess you were kinder to him than to me!"

"Wait!" cried Brogeen. "Wait!"

The Pedlar had flung down the piece of leather. Clasping his hands about his knees, he watched the leprechaun spread it out and measure his own tiny foot against it.

" 'Twill do!" he said at last folding his arms and gazing down at the pedlar, who was gazing up at him. "There's enough for the two of us. I shouldn't make boots for you, but I will! After all—you're a travelling man and no stranger to us!"

"Have it yer own way, so long as 'tis mine," chuckled Peter. "Will I pay ye now or when the boots is finished?"

"Will you let me have a pair of shoes from this leather when I've cut out your own?" demanded Brogeen.

"Bedad I will!" answered the pedlar. " 'Tisn't much leather your shoes will need. Ye can have all that's left."

"That will be payment enough!" the leprechaun told him. "And thank you kindly!"

"When will they be ready?" asked Peter. "Me feet is wore out with these old brogues and—you know the way it is at Easter!"

"Next market day! When the sun strikes the top of the mountain I'll be here with the boots!" promised Brogeen.

He rolled the leather, tucked it under his arm and, without a word of farewell, scuttled up the boreen.

Peter the Pedlar refilled his pack and swung it over his shoulder.

"Mebbe I'm all kinds of a gommie," he said to himself. "Yet, somehow, I don't think I am!"

He strode away and never once looked back.

9

The Green Shoes

rogeen was in such haste he could hardly stop to close the door before he had out the table and his tools and was drawing the shape of a pair of boots big enough for the pedlar.

"I could put him off with shoes!" muttered the leprechaun. "But don't I well know 'tis boots a man needs, snug about his ankles and he marching across the bog and over the mountains. I'll act fair by Peter the Pedlar, if I do have to make my own shoes out of bits and pieces. I wouldn't want him to tell Batt Kelly I didn't treat him decent!"

Brogeen had never attempted so big a job of work before. His tiny hands were aching when he had cut out the boots. He sat down to rest but his fire was only smouldering, so he piled it with wood and filled his kettle.

After a cup of tea, he gathered all the odd scraps of leather, placed them in his chest and began stitching the uppers.

"It would be a great lump of a man like Peter would be wanting me to make boots for him," grumbled the leprechaun. "Let's hope there won't be any orders coming in."

He worked until he fell asleep over his table. In the morning he slept late. The moment he awoke, he ran down to the withered thorn bush at the end of the boreen where the Good People left their work for him.

A roll of blue silk and a folded piece of red felt told him that one of them wanted a pair of dancing shoes and another needed comfortable slippers to wear indoors.

Brogeen screwed up his face crossly as he stared at them.

"Wouldn't you think they'd get tired of dancing and why wouldn't a pair of old shoes do for sitting at the fire! 'Pon me word, I'll have to work day and night the way things are!"

His friend the wren followed him up the boreen.

"Go along like a decent fellow, have your breakfast and scatter the crumbs!" called the bird.

Brogeen nodded and, walking slowly between the wren and the blackbird, told them his troubles.

"You'll need a bit of money in your pocket if you do go on your travels," the wren warned him. "So go easy on the pedlar's boots and make sure of the work you should be doing!"

"I'll keep me word to Peter if I never stir from this boreen!" declared Brogeen. "How can you understand me troubles and difficulties?"

He spoke so fiercely that the two birds fled into the bushes and told the others who lived by the stream the way the leprechaun was behaving.

Every day after breakfast, Brogeen settled to his proper work and kept on until he was starving for his dinner. Then he brought out the pedlar's boots and stitched and hammered until he couldn't sew another stitch or hammer another nail.

Market day came. The leprechaun was out of bed before sunrise. He still had to polish the boots, so that Peter would be the best shod pedlar in the whole of Ireland.

Yawning and shivering he stumbled down the boreen and, as he stepped out to the road, there was Peter striding along and the sun coming up behind him.

The pedlar saw Brogeen standing there, pinched with cold, the heavy boots clasped in his arms.

"You're a great little lad, so you are! I've never had such boots before!" he said. "I'll be a proud and happy man. Look now, I've brought you a present!"

He searched in his pockets and pulled out a pair of buckles set with gleaming green stones.

"They're for your shoes!" he told the leprechaun.

Brogeen raced home longing to begin work. He never thought of looking in the thorn bush.

He laid the buckles on the windowsill where they glittered so that he could have stood admiring them all day. He prepared a whole cauldron full of porridge and, while it was cooking, brought the bundle of pieces from the chest.

"Sure they're just scraps!" grumbled the leprechaun. "Wasn't I very foolish to make boots for that giant of a pedlar! If I'd had sense and given him shoes he'd have been content and I'd have been made up!"

For all his grumblings, by the time the porridge was bubbling, Brogeen had cut out two neat little shoes.

"There'll be a desprit lot of stitching!" he mumbled, his mouth full.

He sprinkled another spoonful of brown sugar on the porridge and wished he had cream or even milk. But he wouldn't spare the time to go for it.

"If I lived up the mountain I'd be better off," he thought. "I'd have comrades to do a hand's turn for me. But I wouldn't leave me house under the beech to be in a palace, that's sure!"

When Brogeen was hungry he ate a saucerful of porridge. When the fire died down, he ran out for an armful of sticks. He didn't even shake up his bed of leaves.

The uppers were made of patches, joined with stitches so fine they were part of the leather. The soles were nailed, layer on layer, until there wasn't a scrap left.

As Brogeen worked he talked to the shoes. He told them about other leprechauns and of life in the Fort of Sheen. He talked to them about Peter the Pedlar and of how they would be with him on their travels. He whispered that they were the loveliest shoes he had ever made and that he was proud of them.

"You're lovelier even than the last shoes I made for the Queen!"

The blackbird came every day to admire the work and when Brogeen was too tired to talk, sang his sweetest songs.

But the wren warned the leprechaun that the withered thorn was choked with rolls of leather and silk and satin. Brogeen wouldn't listen.

"When me shoes is finished I'll turn to them jobs," he said. "Haven't I the right to do something for meself once in a while? I've a great wish to meet Peter the Pedlar the day I start me travels—him in his green boots and me in me lovely green shoes!"

"I'd wish to see the two of you!" whistled the blackbird. "I do appreciate a bit of colour!"

He clacked his beak so that everyone could admire it.

"The bush is a disgrace!" declared the wren. "You should be ashamed! A leprechaun is like a bird or anyone else. If he doesn't do his rightful work, there's trouble."

"Bad cess to you!" growled Brogeen, and he slammed his door. "How could wren understand how I feel about me shoes? the blackbird is different. He knows!"

At last the shoes were finished. Brogeen had only to stitch on the buckles!

"After breakfast in the morning," he said, as

he lay down asleep the moment he snuggled under the rush mat.

The full moon sent a beam through the window and Brogeen, thinking it was morning, rubbed his eyes.

"Bedad 'tis only the moon! I've hours of rest before me!"

He stretched comfortably but he couldn't go to sleep again. A queer scuffling came from the chest.

"You'd think 'twas the wind blowing dried leaves along the bank," he muttered.

"Let me out! Let me out!" called two tiny voices.

Brogeen was frightened. He tiptoed across the room. Something was tapping against the lid of the chest.

He lifted it with trembling fingers and out sprang the two shoes. Before he could stop them they ran to the door, jumped and kicked up the latch. Then out they went, over the stepping stones and along the boreen.

After them ran the leprechaun.

"Come back, me lovely green shoes, 'til I sew the shining buckle on you!"

"Wait now and let me slip into you!"

"We'll travel the roads together!"

"You'll not know where to go without me!"

Dancing, skipping, shuffling—on went the shoes! They left Brogeen far behind. Down the road they ran and the last he saw of them was when they raced over the Bridge of the Seven Arches.

The leprechaun shivered with cold. His bare feet were bruised on the stones and, as he turned back to the boreen, pieces of silk and leather began to fall out of the withered thorn.

"The best shoes I ever made!" he sighed. "And all I have is the pedlar's buckles and the work I've been dodging. I put me own pride into them and dear knows if I'll ever set eyes on them again. Wirra! Wirra!"

10

Runaways

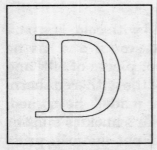

ancing, skipping, shuffling—on went the green shoes! Down the road and over the Bridge of the Seven Arches.

The noise they made echoed beneath them until they were frightened and kept close together, running steadily right, left! right, left! until the bridge was far behind.

The road was muddy, golden scraps of straw and wisps of hay were scattered among the puddles which reflected the cold blue sky. An easterly wind tossed the straw and hay and beat up little waves on the puddles.

The shoes scampered gaily over the straw and hay and around the puddles. When a splash of mud showed on Left-shoe's toe, up he went on the grassy bank to clean it and Right-shoe had to follow. When the toe was rubbed clean, down hopped Left-shoe to the muddy road and along came Right-shoe.

They danced slowly now and, when they came to the cross-roads with a grand new signpost, the shoes stopped in the middle of the road. The post was freshly painted white, so were the arms, but the names weren't there. This made no difference to the shoes. Only when Left-shoe pointed left, Right-shoe pointed right and, as they had to go together, there they stuck.

They had come down the road from the bridge. The left road went to the town, the right to a village. The shoes didn't know this, but Left-shoe wouldn't follow right, and Right-shoe was determined not to follow left. They didn't want to go back, so they kept straight on. Right was persistent. When the road divided he didn't hesitate a moment but trotted smartly to the right and Left meekly followed.

The road became a rough boreen—all stones and puddles.The shoes had to hop and skip and leap. Once Left stubbed his toe on a sharp stone and there was a scratch on the lovely green leather. Right came down in a puddle and was spattered from heel to toe.

The boreen led to a farm-yard—a muddy, untidy, comfortable farm-yard. The gate was open and perched on the top rung was a red cock. He had a gorgeous tail and was so proud he spent his time crowing on the gate, the turf-pile, or the haystack. Sometimes he would leap and flutter to the roof. Then he crowed louder than ever!

He saw the shoes. He had never seen shoes wandering alone before and he didn't understand them. All the shoes he had known had feet in them. And he was more accustomed to boots than shoes, great strong, heavy farm boots, not dainty green shoes.

So he gave out such a cock-a-doodle-do that all the hens, the sow with her long line of bonaveens, the calf, the goat, the dog, came running across the yard to learn the reason for the tumult.

The cat was on the windowsill and never stirred. She was a beautiful ginger cat and a great pet. So she was quite used to boots and shoes without feet in them—wet boots drying by the fire, slippers warming for the evening, shoes being polished for Sunday morning.

"Such a fuss about nothing!" scoffed the ginger cat.

The hens and all the animals of the farmyard stood inside the gate, watching the two green shoes. The boldest hen stepped a little nearer. The shoes began to dance and she scuttled back.

The cock crowed again!

From the back of the turf-pile peeped a little girl. Carmel had been building a house with sods and she was as brown as dry turf mould. Her straight fair hair stood on end. Her little snub nose was inquisitive and covered with pale gold fairy spots.

She saw the cat sitting up on the windowsill.

"What's wrong with cocky?" she asked, running over and stroking Ginger. "Oh, look at the doty green shoes!"

Carmel was barefoot. She liked being barefoot, though she had a very good pair of boots her mother had bought last Fair Day. But they were strong, black, lace boots and she had never seen such beautiful shoes as the two standing side by side at the gate.

She crossed the yard on tiptoe and squeezed in between the calf and the goat.

Carmel stretched out one bare, brown foot.

The shoes were strange in the world. But they understood that once feet were in them, they wouldn't be free to run and dance as they chose.

Right and Left skipped back, turned round

and raced off down the rough, stony boreen.
After them went Carmel.

"They're lovely shoes!" she thought. "I never
knew shoes could run by themselves. I wish
they were mine! I wish daddy would come!
He'd catch them for me!"

The shoes tried to avoid the puddles and the
sharp stones. They weren't used to being
chased. They weren't used to running along a
stony, muddy boreen.

The little girl was. She could run anywhere,
and she was gaining on the shoes!

Carmel stooped and reached out. Her
fingers nearly touched Left-shoe, when Right-
shoe gave a kick that sent him leaping into the
air. Carmel reached again, slipped and fell
face downward in the mud.

"Carmel!" called her mother. "Breakfast's
ready!"

She scrambled up. The shoes were out of the
boreen, racing down the road.

Carmel went back to the farm-house. The
shoes went on.

They passed where the road forked. They
didn't stop but sped on until they reached the
crossroads again.

The road to the village was muddy, not
much better than the boreen which had led

them to the farm-yard and its dangers.
Neither wanted to go that way and both were
determined not to return over the seven-
arched bridge.

The only other way was the road to the
town, a well-made road with high banks.
Though the day was so early, a cart and a man
driving a flock of sheep were travelling to the
town, for this was Fair Day.

The green shoes followed the cart, walking
underneath it. They didn't notice that after
the sheep came a herd of cows, carts piled with
yellow, winter turnips, elegant early cabbage
and fine big old potatoes.

The shoes thought what a decent quiet road
it was. Presently they thought it too quiet.
After that, they longed for a decent quiet road
more than anything in the world!

The road came to the town. The fair was
held in a large field sheltered by a belt of trees.
The cart turned sharply, two sheep ran after it
and, at once, the runaway shoes were in the
middle of the flock. They tried to squeeze
between the thin legs and, at last, with a hop,
skip and a jump, arrived in front of the stall
where a woman was arranging oranges and
apples.

She saw the shoes. They hadn't been there a

moment before, she was sure of that!

"Somebody's dropped them!" declared the fruit woman. "Now who?"

She stared. The shoes were moving. Slowly they walked down the lane between the stalls.

"Will ye look at that!" cried the woman, pointing.

She didn't go after them. She didn't want shoes that walked by themselves!

A boy, wandering along, his hands in his pockets, saw her pointing, saw the shoes. He was sure they didn't belong to her, so there was no reason why they shouldn't belong to him. He walked after them. The shoes began to run. The boy ran. The shoes ran faster!

"That's a clever trick!" declared a man, leaning against a cart.

He followed the shoes and the boy. Soon everyone in the fair was running. The shoes darted under a stall, crept out the other side and ran with the running feet.

All around them muddy boots with thick soles, studded with nails, clattered and stamped. The green shoes were kicked and pushed. Once Left-shoe was trodden on.

They came near the trees. Both decided at the same moment, scurried into the long grass and were safely hidden.

The people who had followed them looked puzzled, strolled back to their business and wondered who was the lucky one who had picked up the magic shoes.

A dog came smelling and sniffing among the trees, so the shoes hurried on. He barked, followed them a little way and trotted back to his master at the fair.

The shoes walked now. They climbed a path which crossed the hill. Beside a rock they came upon two boots, lying empty and forgotten. The green shoes marched proudly by, for the boots were cracked and worn. The path descended the other side to a river crossed by a slippery plank bridge. Creeping and sliding, the shoes nearly fell into the water. It took them a long time but they reached the far bank in safety.

Left, right! Left, right! went the shoes out on the lonely bog. No such shoes had ever been on that bog before! It was growing dark, yet in the bushes and clumps of heather, among the rushes growing in pools—whisperings, chatterings and scurryings followed the runaway shoes. They didn't know where to stop so they kept on.

If they had known the way back to the boreen, the weary shoes might have turned then and gone home to Brogeen and the snug chest. But they weren't only runaways, they were lost!

They went through a village. In the cabins people were sitting by the fire having their tea. Smoke rose from the chimneys and the glow from the hearths shone through windows and over half-doors. The shoes didn't pause, though they might have found a good home in that village. The shadows lengthened. The moon rose and the patter of the shoes on the road was like the sound of dried leaves blown before the north wind.

Towards morning they came to a wide road by a river. They crossed the river by a great bridge, crept along a quay, up a narrow lane and could go no farther.

They were outside a shuttered shop. The smell of leather and polish came from it. Two shallow steps led to the window. The door was fastened but they hopped up. Left wedged into a corner, Right snuggled close to Left, toe to toe, muddy, scuffed, tired.

The green shoes had found a refuge at the door of a cobbler's shop. In the morning he discovered them, gave each a good cleaning and polishing, and set them in his window but in a dark corner where they wouldn't be easily seen.

"They'll be called for!" he told his assistant. "Whoever left them was in a hurry and didn't leave a note, or it might be the note was blown away. They'll be safe enough here!"

The old man stood gazing at them.

"Once I dreamed of making shoes like those," he told the young man who worked with him. "I hoped my shoes would send the people who wore them marching and dancing through life, not shuffling! Ah, well! I'm old now! But you're young! Take a good look at them. Feel the lovely shape and the soft thick leather. Trace the fine stitches!"

"A shoe's a shoe!" declared the young man. "Some are big, some small; some dear, some cheap! That's all there is to it! Now I'd like to make football boots. One touch and the ball would go where the boot pleased. I'd have great fun making those boots!"

The shoes were snug and comfortable. They had nothing to do but sit quietly on their shelf.

Brogeen had told them stories of wanderings on fine roads which led to grand cities and palaces. He had spoken of halls where everyone danced and where they would be admired and cared for.

In this dim shop there were thick hobnail

boots, children's shapeless sandals and strong lace shoes. There wasn't a single pair of dancing shoes in the place!

The cobbler's was at the corner of a busy street but the runaway shoes were at the end of the window facing on a quiet alley. Sometimes a cat sat on the windowsill, inspecting the rows of boots and shoes, when it wasn't washing its handsome black coat. Little boys rolled marbles there and small girls played hop-scotch. They didn't bother to look in at the window. If they had, they couldn't have seen the green shoes.

The green shoes knew they hadn't been made to lie dusty and hidden on a cobbler's shelf. They grew restless. One night they wriggled and pushed and squeezed until, when morning came, they dropped down beside the door.

The cobbler lifted out the bar and the door swung back, letting sunlight stream into the dark shop. The shoes were too clever to move. But when the old man went into the kitchen to fill the kettle and make a cup of tea, the green shoes slipped down the steps out to the street.

Left, right! Left, right! Hop, skip, jump! They were once more on their travels!

11

Neighbours' Advice

rogeen was so unhappy over his lost green shoes that he couldn't take pride in the beautiful buckles the pedlar had given him, but put them away in his chest so that he wouldn't be reminded of his disappointment.

One day Brogeen was trudging home when out fluttered the wren from his crowded nest in the bank.

"How's yourself, Brogeen?" he asked.

"Only middling!" sighed the little shoemaker.

"Only middling!"

"You need a holiday!" declared the wren. "You should have a change. You've done nothing but work and work and work this long while."

"True for you," agreed Brogeen. "But what

else can I do?"

The wren cocked his head on one side and looked up at the leprechaun with bright friendly eyes.

"Usen't you be talking to the blackbird about how you wanted to travel a bit and see the world, or have you forgotten?"

"Whisha!" said the leprechaun, despairingly. "Sure I talked! More's the pity! But don't you know well what happened to the shoes I made to go travelling in? Didn't the blackbird tell you? He knew! And I haven't the heart to set to work on another pair, even if I had the time and the leather."

The wren flapped his wings.

"I've been that busy, I never did get to hearing rightly what happened. We all knew you were making a huge pair of boots for Peter the Pedlar and a pair of travelling shoes for yourself. We were all out watching Peter marching away in his grand green boots for all the world like an Emperor. But we never set eyes on yours, Brogeen. We never saw heel or toe of them!"

Brogeen nodded mournfully.

"Puffed up with pride and conceit, I was! But you would have seen them, Wren, when they were finished. 'Tis yourself and

Blackbird I'd show them to before anyone else!"

He stood thinking of his lost shoes, his head sunk on his chest. "Were they stole on you?" asked the wren, speaking in a whisper.

"They were not!" replied Brogeen. "Who'd steal from a neighbour along our boreen? And never a stranger knew about them. They ran away on me!"

"Ran away!" repeated the wren, very perplexed.

"Ran away!" declared the little shoemaker.

He told the wren every bit about the green shoes from the moment Peter the Pedlar gave him the leather up to the time when the runaways raced across the Bridge of the Seven Arches and vanished.

Brogeen wept. But he didn't feel nearly so unhappy. When he had finished and wiped his eyes with the end of his muffler, he discovered that all the neighbours had left their work to listen to his troubles. The hedge sparrows perched on the bushes, the thrushes sat down in the grass away from the wind, a tit turned somersaults on the long swaying branch of a willow powdered with gold. The blackbird strutted up and down, while his quiet wife kept very still in the old ash, as they heard about the green shoes.

"What should he do?" asked the wren softly, looking with his bright little eyes from one neighbour to another.

All the beaks opened together and shut as suddenly

"I!" exclaimed one sparrow.

"I! I! I!" cried all the other sparrows.

"If you were to ask me," said the biggest and fattest of the thrushes.

"We are asking you!" snapped the wren.

He was disappointed. The neighbours weren't nearly as clever as he had hoped.

The blackbird rubbed his golden beak on the bark of the ash, flew up, whistling a few gay notes and settled beside his wife.

"What should Brogeen do, my dear?" he asked. "You tell him."

Kind, friendly Mrs Blackbird sat there thinking hard. All the other birds were looking at her but she didn't mind. She smoothed her tail feathers, shook her wings and fluttered off. Over her shoulder she called—

"Follow the shoes Never give in! Follow the shoes!"

"Follow the shoes!" twittered the sparrows. "Follow the shoes, Brogeen!"

Off they flew, chattering and twittering, delighted with themselves.

"Just as I told you!" cried the big thrush. All the other thrushes carolled "Just as we told you!"

The blackbird gave a whistle like a clear mocking laugh and darted away.

Brogeen and the wren were alone.

"How can I go without proper travelling shoes!" grumbled the leprechaun.

He started as a queer noise and a splashing came from a marshy corner of the stream. A clump of rushes grew there and, one hot summer day, Brogeen had caught sight of a blue dragon-fly hovering above them.

But no dragon-fly ever made such a noise. He was sure of that!

The wren put his head on one side and watched the rushes.

"Listening!" he said, indignantly. "I'd be ashamed!"

A green frog poked out his head. He yawned until Brogeen feared he would split in two.

"Why shouldn't I listen?" he croaked. "I suppose you wanted me to come out and face sparrows, blackbirds and thrushes—crowds and swarms of them! Have sense, wren, do!"

The wren looked very offended.

"You've no manners, no manners at all, let me tell you!" he said. "And now you have come out of hiding, what do you want?"

"I was sitting up on the middle stepping stone last night when two owls flew overhead. And do you know what the big owl said to the little owl?"

"Sure, how could we know?" demanded Brogeen.

The frog goggled his eyes.

"The big owl said to the little owl—"when Brogeen of the Stepping Stones meets the Speckled Horse of Waterford, the Pig Cart of Dungarvan and the Shadow Pedlar on the one day, he's caught up with the green shoes"!"

"Are you sure you heard it? I mean, 'twasn't a dream you were after having?" demanded Brogeen.

The frog opened his mouth, leaped in the air, clapped his long thin hind legs together and landed with a splash at the far side of the rushes.

"Dream!" he croaked. "Do I look the kind of chap that would sit on a stepping stone dreaming of owls?"

Brogeen marched up the boreen.

"I'll have to work every hour of the day!" he said. "But I'll do all there is to be done, pack

me tools and away with me. Haven't I been
very foolish to waste all this time. 'Twill be
terrible to catch up with them shoes and me in
me old brogues!"

The wren flew away and every time he
stopped he spoke to a sparrow. The sparrows
didn't fly far but each one, when it stopped
spoke to another and as they flew they
twittered continually—

> "Brogeen of the Stepping Stones
> Is going away.
> Do not leave work for him,
> After today."

The next morning when Brogeen went down
the boreen and looked at the deserted
blackbird's nest in the thorn bush, it was
empty.

"That's queer!" declared the little
shoemaker. "Queer but grand. Sure, I'm made
up with nothing to do!"

He put new thick soles on his brogues, tidied
the house, polished his hammer, his scissors,
his knife and rolled them in his apron. The box
which held needles, thread and nails, he
tucked into the deep pocket of his coat. He
cleaned his cauldron and hung it over the

empty grate, first putting away a few gold coins for special gifts as well as the ordinary money he had earned in the town by making children's shoes.

He was taking a last look round when suddenly he darted to the chest, lifted the lid, and took out the sparkling buckles Peter the Pedlar had given him.

"Wasn't I nearly forgetting!" thought Brogeen.

He opened the door.

"'Twill be a long time before I walk in here again," said the leprechaun. "Now what's all the noise about?"

He had never heard such a commotion in his life but there were friends and acquaintances from over the mountain and the wood, where Brogeen collected his sticks; squirrels, the water rat, a badger, the frog from the rushes were crowding the stepping stones, the bank and the bushes, pushing, squeezing so that it was a mercy most of them had wings!

Brogeen had to force his way through the throng.

"Happy journey! Happy journey!" whistled the blackbird.

"Safe home! Safe home!" chirped the sparrows.

"Sure I haven't even started!" protested Brogeen.

"Remember me to-to-to—" said the big thrush, looking very important.

"See all you can! See all you can!" advised Mrs Blackbird.

The frog hopped back among the rushes. He wasn't too happy with so many birds about. The squirrel began looking for a store of nuts he thought were hidden near the beech. He wanted to give them to his friends. Mrs Blackbird went home to her three children. Soon only the blackbird and the wren were left.

"You'll keep an eye on me house?" asked Brogeen.

"Don't bother your head about anything!" the wren told him.

" 'Twill be lonesome without you," said the blackbird thoughtfully. "But I'll be wondering about your coming home and us listening to all your grand adventures."

"With the green shoes!" added Brogeen.

12

Over the Bridge

 rogeen stepped out of the boreen between the white and the black thorn bushes on to the road.

He looked back. The blackbird danced on the blackthorn, whistling a gay little tune. The wren chirped sadly.

The blackbird fluttered into the air as if he were going too. Brogeen stopped for a moment to listen to the blackbird's song—

"I'll fly away
One day.
Far, far, far!

"Where will I fly?
To where the sky
Falls, falls, falls!

"Then I will come
Back home,
Tired, tired, tired!"

The blackbird dropped down on the thorn. The wren flapped his wings. Brogeen waved his hand and trotted off towards the Bridge of the Seven Arches.

"If only I had me lovely green shoes!" he sighed.

But the sun was rising in the sky and the road was downhill. If the wind had a bite in it, that was all the better for walking. Brogeen's legs weren't long and his feet weren't big but surely he could go as fast as the green shoes! Hadn't he made them?

Only they were days ahead of him!

When he came to the crossroads, he was curious. Why hadn't he explored all these roads? The leprechaun had never been so far, except on market or fair days, when it was easy to ride on a cart or horse, or even perch on the back of a bicycle.

Today the road was empty. Brogeen had seen the green shoes crossing the bridge, so he knew he was on the right track. He kept on until he came to the crossroads before the town.

"Three roads to choose from," he muttered. "Now would them runaways go to the town or wouldn't they?"

By this time he was hungry, for he had been too excited to bother about breakfast. In his pocket he had a piece of bread and cheese and he sat on the sunny side of the road to eat it.

"If only I had a sup of milk or cider," he grumbled. " 'Tis dry work eating without drinking."

"Good morning, little man!" said a voice. "I'm Carmel! What's your name?"

Brogeen looked up in alarm. He saw a little barefoot girl, with straight fair hair, a jolly snub nose covered with fairy spots and the friendliest smile he had ever seen.

He knew he needn't be afraid of Carmel! She carried a big billycan of milk, and, as she spoke, set it down with a splash.

"Good morning to you, Carmel!" returned the shoemaker. "Me name's Brogeen. I'm pleased to know you. Will you have a morsel of bread and cheese?"

Carmel nodded. She had eaten her breakfast, but it seemed a long time ago and Brogeen's bread and cheese looked much nicer than the bread and cheese they had at the farm. She settled herself beside him, felt in the pocket of her pinny and pulled out two tiny wooden cups. She filled them with milk from the billycan and handed one to Brogeen.

"I'll give you the cup for a present," said Carmel. "I've lost the doll it belonged to."

The milk was still warm and foaming. The bread was fresh, the crumb soft, with a thick, crisp crust, and the cheese was like cream.

Brogeen and Carmel, eating and drinking in the sunshine, were so happy they didn't bother to talk. When the last scrap was eaten and they had each drunk three cupfuls of milk, Brogeen brushed the crumbs from his muffler, put the wooden cup in his pocket and stood up.

"Thank you kindly, Carmel! I must be on me way. I'm following a pair of green shoes and they have the start on me."

"Green shoes!" cried Carmel. "I know them! They came to the farm. They ran away and I couldn't catch them. I fell in the mud and bumped my knee. That was a long time ago!"

Brogeen was very excited. "Which road did they take?" he asked.

Carmel shook her head.

"I didn't see. But it was Fair Day so I expect they went to the fair. Goodbye, Brogeen. I'm going to the village!"

"Goodbye, Carmel, and thank you kindly for the cup!"

She picked up the billycan and ran off. As Brogeen went slowly towards the town, he heard the tramp of horse's hoofs and the jangling of harness. He looked back and saw a hay wagon coming down the road. He stepped behind a bush until it had almost passed, then swung up and settled himself in the hay.

"Sure, this is the way to travel!" he thought. "Still, 'tis desperate slow. I'll never catch up on me green shoes!"

But he was very comfortable. He leaned back, stretched his legs and, because he was tired and the jogging of the cart rocked him gently, he fell asleep.

The cart swung round so suddenly that, as Brogeen woke, he was nearly thrown off. He clutched at a rope and slipped to the ground. The big grey horse had pulled up in a narrow turning by a boot shop Brogeen knew well. The door was wide open and the shop-keeper lounged there, gazing across the main street.

He didn't see Brogeen and presently began to clean the window with a big duster.

"He'd be the one to notice a pair of green shoes," thought Brogeen. "But I daren't ask him. Isn't he the one that called me a thief and ran me!"

So he went on to the Fair Green. A boy was sitting against the wall, with a pile of dry branches beside him, breaking them into firewood. He whistled as he worked and Brogeen liked the look of him. He stopped in front of the boy and waited.

At last the boy saw him.

"Hallo!" he said. "Are you good at breaking sticks?"

"Only middling," replied Brogeen. "I'm a shoemaker meself."

"A shoemaker!" repeated the boy, gazing at his feet which were bare. "I nearly had a pair of shoes. You never saw such shoes! Green ones, they were! I almost had them, last Fair Day!"

"And you lost them?" asked Brogeen. "That was hard!"

"I didn't lose them, because I never had them," explained the boy. "Mind you, they were strange shoes. They went by themselves! Everybody in the fair was chasing them, so I hadn't any chance. I wonder where they are now!"

He stood up, shaded his eyes from the sun and pointed at the belt of trees beyond the green.

"That's the way they went," he said. "I saw them in among the trees. But when I tried to find them they were gone. I might have sold them and bought a pair of boots that would go where I wanted. Though I think I'd have kept those shoes. They were too lovely to sell!"

"Good luck to you," said Brogeen. "I'll be on me way!"

The little shoemaker followed the path through the wood. As he came from the shelter of the trees he saw how the path climbed a steep hill. It was a bare hill with tangled bushes and heather but not a single tree. They had all been cut down. Sheep were scattered on the smooth patches of grass. They cropped without ceasing for a moment and not even the nearest raised its head when Brogeen called out—

"Did any of you see a pair of green shoes travelling this way a while back?"

He leaned against a tree and waited patiently. All he heard was. the biting and tearing of grass—munch, munch, munch!

"Never did think a whole lot of sheep!" said Brogeen loudly.

Even that didn't make them turn round. But a scuffling and chattering above his head made Brogeen look up.

Half-hidden behind a clump of leaves, a red squirrel was peeping down at him from an overhanging branch.

"Did I hear you mention green shoes?" asked the squirrel shyly.

"You did!" answered Brogeen.

His sharp voice terrified the squirrel, who flattened himself against the tree, while his ruddy, bushy tail waved and quivered.

"Whisha! What call have I to be screeching at the poor little fella and him only trying to help me? Don't I know how nervous squirrels are!" thought the leprechaun.

"Hi!" he called. "I did mention green shoes! Don't mind me shocking manners. I'm vexed and annoyed. Not with anybody but meself. I made those green shoes and I lost them. I've follyed them this far and I'll folly 'til I come up with them!"

The squirrel poked out his head. "What will you do then?" Brogeen was puzzled.

"What will I do? Why, put them on me two feet! What else would I do? Aren't they mine? Didn't I make them? They're the shoes I meant to travel in and see the big world!"

The squirrel nibbled a nut and looked thoughtful.

"I didn't know they were travelling shoes.

They looked like dancing shoes."

"Mebbe they were and mebbe they weren't!" muttered Brogeen. "But I made them. And now if you wouldn't mind telling me which way they went I'd be greatly obliged."

"Up over the hill," the squirrel was saying, when Brogeen heard a creaking, grunting, wheezing kind of noise that made him dart in among the trees.

"What is it?" he asked the squirrel in a whisper.

13

The Onion Woman

s the noise came nearer it made the little shoe-maker wish he couldn't hear at all.

"It must be a terrible fearsome creature!" he thought. "Mebbe I'd as well get up aloft there!"

Yet the squirrel went on cracking and nibbling as if he didn't hear a sound.

"What is it?" demanded Brogeen again, so fiercely the squirrel dropped his nut and jumped down to find it.

Brogeen picked up the nut.

"Will you, or won't you, tell me what strange animal is making them desprit noises?" he asked, handing back the nut.

"'Tis only the onion woman driving by with her onions," answered the squirrel leaping gaily back into the tree.

Brogeen peered out.

Along a rough track which kept to the shelter of the trees, came the oldest, most broken-down cart he had ever seen. It was drawn by a rough-coated little pony, whose head drooped mournfully. Every bit of the cart grumbled and groaned. No wonder Brogeen had been alarmed.

A fat sleepy untidy woman slumped on the seat dozing. She wore a tattered red petticoat and was wrapped in a dilapidated black shawl. Behind her the cart was piled with onions—big, brown, gleaming onions.

"Would you be kind enough to give me a lift, ma'am?" asked Brogeen.

"Sure there's plenty of room for two," she answered sleepily. "Come along up and welcome."

The pony was going so slowly Brogeen pulled himself up without much trouble, settled on the seat, folded his arms and gazed around.

"Wrong way!" chattered the squirrel. "Path over the hill! Green shoes went over the hill!"

He leaped from tree to tree, chattering as he leaped. The wind carried to Brogeen the squirrel's warning—

"Wrong way! Over the hill! Over the hill!" until Brogeen could hear him no longer.

"'Tis true I wanted them shoes to go travelling in," said the leprechaun to himself. "Only didn't I make up me mind to go travelling before I met Peter the Pedlar? If the green shoes want to climb hills, let them! They'll be tired before I am!"

He wanted to sing but he wasn't sure the onion woman would like his voice, so he kept silent.

They left the trees behind and crossed the slope of the hill towards a wide road.

The pony pushed out through a gap in the stone wall and, if the cart had groaned when it was on the track, it groaned more than ever on the road. The pony sighed and grunted and snorted as if it were a cart-load of pigs going to the market.

"'Tis a grand day, thanks be to God!" said the onion woman.

"'Tis indeed!" agreed Brogeen. "But what ails the pony, ma'am? Is he in trouble?"

The onion woman pulled her ragged black shawl closer for, if the sun was shining, the wind was bitter as ice!

"'Tis his feet, the crathure!" she said. "And I don't know why! Hasn't he four splendid new shoes on him?"

"I'm a bit of a shoemaker meself, ma'am,"

said Brogeen. "Though I don't set out to make them for the likes of him. Will you pull up and let me see can I do anything at all?"

The onion woman pulled up and Brogeen climbed down. He lifted the pony's legs one by one. The pony nuzzled the leprechaun's shoulder and sighed deeply.

"You poor thing!" said Brogeen. "The shoes are good enough but they're on back to front! I'll fix that!"

The onion woman's eyes opened very wide when Brogeen unfastened his bag and she saw the wonderful tools. She said nothing, shut her mouth very tight, then nodded thoughtfully.

Brogeen took off the shoes and replaced them properly. The pony felt so comfortable he started off before the leprechaun could sit down and sent him toppling. Brogeen clutched the onion woman's shawl but it was so worn it tore and, if he hadn't fallen against the side of the cart, he would have been out on the roadway.

"There's gratitude!" he exclaimed indignantly. "There's consideration for you!"

"Sure, poor Dan avic meant no harm," said the onion woman. "Ye made him so, he doesn't know what to do with himself. Isn't he the lucky one? I've me toes out through me boots these weeks and dear knows how I'll walk in them!"

She groaned and then chuckled.

"Does it matter what class of boots I'm wearing an' I cocked up in the cart? Isn't it a grand little cart I have? Did ye ever see a finer one? Tell me now!"

Brogeen looked at the cart. It was a wreck! There were holes in the floor and sacks laid over them to keep the onions from falling through. The seat wouldn't have supported the onion woman, only for the box under it. The shafts were mended with wire and string, the wheels were bound with strips of sacking to keep them together. The leprechaun was mostly very truthful, so he didn't answer.

The onion woman was offended. She was very proud of her cart. She tossed her head and her last hairpin slipped out, so that her coil of hair dropped over her shoulder.

Instead of being annoyed she began to laugh.

Her laugh was so loud and jolly it made Brogeen laugh too. Dan avic neighed with delight. The seat thumped against the box, the shafts creaked, the wheels rattled and the blustering wind blew along behind them.

"What name is on ye, little fella?" asked the onion woman, when they had stopped laughing.

"Brogeen, ma'am!"

"Ah, ha! Brogeen the shoemaker! I've heard tell of ye. The best shoemaker in all Ireland! What brings ye abroad? Surely ye have enough work to keep ye home?"

"I have indeed!" declared the leprechaun proudly. "Only I wanted to see the world. I made a pair of travelling shoes and they ran away on me, so I'm following them up!"

"Did they take this way?" asked the onion woman.

Brogeen shook his head.

"They took the path over the hill, so they did!"

"That's a terrible steep hill!" said the onion woman, looking over to where it rose, blue and gaunt against the pearly sky.

"It is!" agreed Brogeen.

"If I could, I'd drive up and over it," she told him. "Still, where'd be the use? They'd be over the other side be this time!"

"And further!" added Brogeen.

"If ye keep on long enough yer road must cross theirs, be raison of the world being round," remarked the onion woman.

"Moreover if 'tis to see the world ye started travelling, ye'll see it better riding in comfort than trapesing in the dust like an old lad of the roads. Isn't it terrible now! I'm parched with the drought and starved with the hunger!"

"I could do with a cut of soda bread and butter, and a sup of tea," said Brogeen hopefully.

"Listen now," said the onion woman. "There's a great little village we're coming to. Let ye fill the basket we're knocking our feet against wid me lovely onions, and go into Aloysius Horan's stores and tell him the onion woman needs he knows what. If ye'll do that, we'll not be starved or parched much longer!"

Brogeen almost stuck out his chest and said—

"Ma'am, I'm a shoemaker, not a higgler, nor yet a huckster!"

But the onion woman looked at him with such a merry grin and winked so gaily, he picked up the basket and, leaning over the seat, gathered handfuls of onions until the basket was filled.

14

Hard Work!

s Brogeen piled on the last onion they drove up the village street and stopped outside a clean, tidy shop with ALOYSIUS HORAN—CHANGE HERE painted over the window.

The window wasn't very big but it was crowded with tins—tins of herrings, tins of salmon, tins of pineapple, tins of peas and, right in the middle, a cardboard box with straw in it. Nestling in the straw were six big, beautiful duck eggs, two green, two blue and two white.

"I'd love a green egg!" thought Brogeen, as he went into the shop.

Inside it was dark and, at first, the leprechaun thought the place was empty. But a long, lean man, with a round red face and white hair standing up in a plume, leaned across the counter and asked very politely, "What can I change for you, sir?"

Brogeen pushed over the basket of onions.

"These are from the onion woman and she bade me say she needs you know what!"

The long thin man smiled very understandingly.

"Lave it to me, sir!" he said. "Lave it to me!"

Brogeen saw that along the counter people were pushing over all kinds of goods and getting others in exchange. No one paid any money and the little shoemaker thought how sensible they were.

An old man gave a bundle of rushes and received a new clay pipe, with a handful of nuts. A little boy, standing on tiptoe, changed a bag of sheep's wool for a pair of gaily coloured stockings and a twist of sweets.

Brogeen would have liked to stay watching. But the friendly man with the rosy face put the onion basket back on the counter. Instead of onions it now held a blue bag of sugar, a red packet of tea, a soda square, a paper of butter and two duck eggs, one blue, one green.

"It was a green egg, I think, sir?" he whispered. "Herself always likes a blue one."

"Thank you kindly," said Brogeen, delighted with his shopping.

He was proud as he went back to the onion woman.

"Whisha! He's forgotten the blackcurrant jam!" she cried. "Give the robber another basket of onions. He'll ruinate me, so he will!"

"I needn't fill it up, need I?" asked Brogeen.

"Bedad, ye must! That's the rule! The basket of onions for what I need. Dear knows, I need me blackcurrant jam!"

"I wonder was it the green egg upset the arrangement?" thought Brogeen.

This time he had to wait while two little girls, who brought in a basket of small green apples, were given a dressed doll each. They were indeed pleased and so was the leprechaun when he saw that as well as the blackcurrant jam, he had a piece of cheese and two Peggy's Legs.

As he climbed back to the cart he noticed that all along the street, people were darting in and out of the cabins, carrying clothes, furniture, sods of turf, logs of wood, even hens and ducks.

"They're terrible busy people!" he said.

"Why wouldn't they be?" asked the onion woman. "If you had to change everything you had, every day, you'd be kept busy, me boyo!"

"But why?" demanded Brogeen. "There's no

sense in changing everything!"

"Sure—'tis the rule!" she explained. "Ye can't go agin the rule! 'Tis hard on the ones that live here but grand for the likes of us!"

Outside the village they came to a little wooded glade with a stream flowing through. A high bank and a fallen tree protected a smooth stretch of grass from the wind, while the sun shone straight down on it.

"Here's a good, snug place for a rest," declared the onion woman. "Tell me, Brogeen, are ye any sort of a hand wid a fire?"

"Is it me?" demanded the little shoemaker. "Let me tell you, I never yet met another that could light a fire to equal me!"

"I believe ye!" she said, urging Dan avic away from the road.

The leprechaun unharnessed the pony, so that he could graze and have a taste of freedom. He gathered sticks and made a fire, broke branches and laid them across the flame until the glade was as snug as a warm kitchen.

The onion woman had a kettle and a saucepan. Brogeen made tea in the kettle and boiled the duck eggs in the saucepan. From her bag the onion woman brought out a cup, a plate, a knife, a spoon. The leprechaun had only the little wooden cup Carmel had given him.

"'Tis easy seeing you're not used to travelling," said the onion woman "Now where's the use of a small cup that size?"

"You'd be surprised what that cup can hold!" Brogeen told her.

They had sweet tinned milk in their tea. Brogeen didn't care much for that but his manners were too good for him to say a word.

"'Tisn't only manners," thought Brogeen. "If I so much as mention milk, that one would be sending me on the search for a cow, or mebbe a wild goat."

The green duck egg was like cream, the white firm, the yolk not soft, not quite hard. The onion woman had a little canister of salt, so not a thing was lacking.

Brogeen had never eaten such bread and butter and the spoonful of blackcurrant jam she laid on it made him feel ready to do any work she wanted.

He leaned back, warm and pleasantly tired.

"Look at them two boots!" said the onion woman, sticking out her feet.

Brogeen looked.

"Can you wonder I don't be prancing up and down, in and out of me cart?" she asked. "I'd be ashamed to have a neighbour, let alone a stranger, set eyes on them. Didn't I hear you say you were a shoemaker?"

"Don't you know well I am!" answered Brogeen with a deep sigh.

"But I suppose you're one of them that's too proud to do a job of patching and mending? You must work on the best, the very best! And a poor, hard-working lassie like meself has to go crippled in boots a self-respecting scarecrow would not be seen in!"

"I'll mend them!" Brogeen told her. "Hand them over!"

While he worked, the onion woman slept. The leprechaun didn't like mending and patching but he made a grand job of the boots. As he set them beside her, the onion woman opened her eyes.

"I'm dreaming!" she declared.

"Try them on!" advised Brogeen.

She pulled on the boots and leaned back, admiring them.

"I always did say I had as neat a foot as any woman in the country if I had me rights," said the onion woman.

Brogeen carefully wrapped his tools in the leather apron and stowed them away in his bag.

"Only I never had me rights," she went on.

"Until I fell in wid the grandest shoemaker ever known!"

"Oh!" cried Brogeen, so confused with delight he dropped his bag and all the tools rolled out.

The onion woman picked them up for him.

"You're a little gentleman!" she said. "That's what you are. When I go home to me old fella that grows the onions and he sees me boots, he won't have a minute's rest or peace until you do the same for him!"

"When are you going home?" asked Brogeen.

"When I sell the last of me onions, back we go! And be that same token we haven't sold the first of them yet, and they the autumn's harvesting. Up and off wid us!"

The fire had died down. Brogeen scattered the ashes, repacked the basket, helped the onion woman back into the cart, harnessed Dan avic, climbed in himself and shook the reins. The sun was out of sight behind the trees, shadows lay across the road but the sky was still radiant and the clouds were crimson and gold.

Brogeen was sleepy. He put the reins in the onion woman's hands. Her fingers clutched them as her eyes closed. He slipped over the seat, put his bag of tools under his head, drew an old sack over him and slept, snug and sound.

He woke once and saw the moon riding overhead. The road glittered, the stone walls were sprinkled with points of light.

"That's a fine, hardy night!" murmured Brogeen.

He snuggled his knees up to his chin and slept again.

Next time it was the mist woke him. A lacy veil of mist that floated above the road from the bog, draped Dan avic in a fleecy mantle and settled over Brogeen and the onions.

"'Twill soon be morning," Brogeen told himself. "I could drop out now and go me own way. Yet somehow I'd like to see that one started on her road home. Sure she hasn't much sense, though she knocks out a good time. I'll hold on a bit longer."

The leprechaun didn't sleep again. Sun and wind between them sent the mist charging away, so that as Brogeen peeped out, he saw great galleons sailing past, galloping unicorns, shadowy boys and girls dancing hand in hand. When the air was clear there was warmth even in the wind.

Brogeen pushed aside the sack and sat up

with the onion woman. She still clutched the reins and, though she slept, she was smiling.

The wind wrapped them in a scent of growing grass, wet turf mould and the salt tang of the sea.

"She hasn't got rid of an onion yet, barring the ones changed in the village," thought Brogeen.

Dan avic wandered from one side of the road to the other, snatching mouthfuls of grass. Now they came out on the bog and passed piles of brown sods and carts half-loaded. Cabins, no bigger than the turf-piles, were scattered along the road and, at the door of one, a man stood smoking his pipe.

A thin trickle of smoke spiralled above his head and, higher up, a fluttering banner streamed from a cabin chimney.

"How's herself?" asked the man. "You're a stranger! I haven't seen you before. Have you a hank of onions? The missis could do with a hank."

Brogeen shook his head.

"They're loose!" he answered. "Just as you see them." The man took the pipe from his mouth and gazed at it.

"I made up my mind I wouldn't take them again unless they were ready to hang up," he said. "But if they're not, they're not! I'll take the basket full."

Brogeen began putting onions into the basket.

"Would five pence be right d'ye think?" asked the man.

"Not a penny less than seven and a half!" declared the onion woman without opening her eyes. "You should know that!"

"Only if they were hanked!" protested the man.

"I'd be ashamed!" exclaimed the onion woman. "Idling there and expecting a poor, hard-working woman to hank the onions for ye!"

"Ah, well!" laughed the man, as he handed over the seven and a half pence. "They're good onions!"

"The best in all Ireland, and not another onion to be found in fair or market at this time of year!" boasted the onion woman.

At the next cabin the woman who looked at them over the half-door refused to take onions unless they were ready to hang on a nail.

"Sure I can't drive Dan avic and rope onions at one and the same time!" protested the onion woman. "You'll have to oblige me, Brogeen!"

The leprechaun sat all day in the back of the

cart plaiting onions on to thick pieces of string. They went through four villages and, by the time they had crossed the bog and reached the great river, the onions were all sold.

"You'll be turning back now?" asked the leprechaun, as he swept the cart clear of onion skins.

"Time enough! Time enough!" declared his companion. "I promised the old fella at home I'd have the cart painted and fixed before I saw him again. I wouldn't want to disappoint him. Are ye any good at the painting, Brogeen?"

The leprechaun's back was aching and his fingers were sore.

"No good at all!" he replied firmly.

They drank milk and ate bread and cheese, sitting up in the cart. The last crumb was finished as they came to the fair of Kilkevin. The onion woman loved fairs. So did Brogeen.

But, as they swung into the market place, he poked a piece of gold into the onion woman's basket and slipped to the ground.

"You're a great wumman!" he thought. "And good company! Only well I know, if I stayed with you, before I'd finished, not to mind painting and fixing the cart, I'd be darning the shawl and patching the petticoat—and me a shoemaker!"

15

The Jolly Beggarman

rogeen went through
the Fair in a great
hurry, yet found time to
buy a saucepan filled with apples as well as a
flat cake of soda bread and a wedge of cheese.

The road went beside the river and the
leprechaun was gazing in wonder at a
steamboat, while overhead an aeroplane
swept through the air like a silver bird.

"Now I am seeing the world!" said Brogeen.

A man, sitting on a log at the water's edge,
stood up, took off his hat and made a low bow.

"Would you help a poor man on his way,
kind sir?" he said.

Brogeen couldn't take off his cap, because
the saucepan, with the apples and cheese, was
under one arm, his bag hung under the other
and the cake of bread was so large he had to
hold it with both hands. For the same reasons,

he couldn't bow properly. But he did his best.

"You're like myself—a traveller !" declared the stranger. "Only you're loaded. I travel easy!"

Brogeen liked his merry face and red hair. There was so much of it, a bunch stuck up through the crown of his tall hat. He wore a black coat buttoned to the chin and, though he had a shoe on one foot and a boot on the other, both were good.

"Might I ask where you're bound for?" said the man politely.

"I'm on me travels!" the leprechaun told him.

"And how far would you be travelling, sir?"

Brogeen stood still and considered. A motor came rushing along the road. The stranger caught the leprechaun by the arm and jumped with him to the grassy bank. They would both have rolled into the river, only the red-haired man clutched at the branch of a tree and pulled them up at the edge.

"Whisha, them road dragons is terrible fierce!" exclaimed Brogeen.

He was trembling and had to sit down.

"What you need is a good, strong cup of tea!" his companion told him. "Sit there! I'll see to everything!"

He searched under the roots of the tree which had saved them. Out came a couple of tins and a few bricks. Set on edge, the bricks made a neat little fireplace. He broke twigs, crumpled a piece of paper, put on larger bits of wood and had a fire blazing as quickly as Brogeen himself could have done. He filled one of the cans with water and was about to set it on the fire, when Brogeen emptied his apples on the grass and held out his saucepan.

"Make the tea in that!" he said.

The redheaded man took a newspaper from his pocket and spread it on the grass for a tablecloth. He had a little bottle of milk and a tin with sugar and tea mixed in it. Brogeen had scarcely time to cut the bread and cheese, and pile the apples in the centre of the newspaper before the saucepan of tea was ready.

The red-haired man drank from a tin. The leprechaun used his wooden cup.

"That's mighty small!" objected the stranger. "You're not having a fair share."

Brogeen grinned.

"Change over and see!"

The red-haired man laughed, took the wooden cup and began to sip the hot tea. He thought he'd need to fill it three or four times to get one drink. Yet there he sat, sipping and sipping, while Brogeen emptied the tin and filled it again.

"That's not an ordinary cup!" said the man. "It's in my mind you're not an ordinary traveller yourself. Now me—I'm a beggarman! What are you?"

"A shoemaker!" replied Brogeen. "And, for your kindness, I'll make that shoe and boot into a pair. There's good leather in them. They're worth me labour! You asked me to help you on your way. That's the best I can do and a good best it is!"

The beggarman took the biggest of the apples in his hands, gave it a squeeze, and it broke in two as if cut with a sharp knife. He gave one half to Brogeen and put the other in his mouth.

"Now this is the rights of it," he said, with his mouth full. "If I had on a pair of shoes, or a pair of boots, no matter how old and broken— who'd notice me? But one boot and one shoe— God pity the poor lad! Think they. We'll have to give him a bit of help!"

The leprechaun sat nibbling the apple. It was sour, but so juicy, he seemed to be drinking cider. When the beggarman had swallowed the last of the apple, he flung back his head and sang, *I am a Little Beggarman.*

"Is it much of a trade?" asked Brogeen.

"Trade indeed! 'Tis a profession! The best of all professions!" cried the red-haired man. "A good beggarman must have manners, a long memory, a knowledge of human nature and a kind heart!"

The leprechaun smiled.

"You have them all, that's sure!" he said. "I must be on me way. I'd like to cross the river. Good luck now!"

"I'll be seeing you!" said the beggarman.

The leprechaun hadn't walked far when a side-car came speeding along the road. He stepped on the grass when the driver called to him. "Are ye wanting a lift to Cloneytubber— me little fella?"

He reached down a hand and, once more, Brogeen was up out of the dust and weariness of the road.

Before the horse could restart, a shout came from the riverside and a stout man, with a peaked cap, came hurrying after them.

"Can you put me on my way, my good man?" he asked breathlessly. "If I'm late for the boat at Cloneytubber, I'll be destroyed. They have my bag, my telescope and my compass on board."

"Jump up!" replied the driver cheerfully. "I always did like a bit of company. I see you're a seafaring chap!"

"Captain!" said the newcomer, proudly.

"Steam?" asked the driver, respectfully.

"Sail!" replied the Captain.

"I'd love to be a sailor!" sighed Brogeen. "Only for a day or two," he added hastily. "Would there be ere a chance of a job on your ship, mister?"

"Can you hoist a sail?" demanded the captain.

Brogeen shook his head.

"Can you coil a rope?"

"I might! If 'twasn't too thick or too long!"

"There are no mights or ifs on the sea!" growled the Captain.

"I wonder could you get up a bit more speed?" he asked the driver. "I'll be in a desperate fix if I don't catch the boat."

"'Tis a comfortable old mare I have. She makes her own pace," explained the driver. "She wouldn't alter it not even for the Captain of a steamboat! God bless her!"

"Maybe I should have hired a motor!" grumbled the Captain.

They talked and argued. Brogeen held on to the back of the seat and looked happily about him. He wondered where were the green shoes.

"Let's hope they're taking care of themselves," he thought. "Now if I'd follyed them, I'd never be having the grand times I am having."

"Were you ever on the salt sea?" he asked the Captain.

"Ever on the salt sea!" exclaimed the Captain. "I've been on every sea and ocean in the world! I've been in storms and shipwrecks. I've been cast on a desert island and then you rise up and ask if I've been on the salt sea!"

"We're coming into Cloneytubber!" interrupted the driver. "We've made grand time. Cast your eye over the boats, Captain, and see if the one you're bound for is still there!"

"It is not!' said the Captain bitterly. "There it goes sailing way with my bag, my telescope and my compass!"

The side-car was rattling along by a little harbour where rowing and sailing boats were moored. A boat was sailing out as the side-car stopped and Brogeen felt sorry for the Captain.

"He's worse off than I was when the green shoes ran away on me," thought the leprechaun.

"I'll consider what I must do," said the Captain. "Only I need rest and a good dinner."

"Here's the best hotel in all Ireland," said the driver. "The landlady's me own sister and we'll be proud to do all we can for ye!"

Brogeen scrambled to the ground.

"Thank you kindly for the lift," he said.

The driver didn't hear him. He was bowing the Captain in through he doorway of the hotel.

As the door closed Brogeen started forward.

"I must be dreaming!" he told himself. "But that grand Captain was wearing one boot and one shoe, and his hair was red! Only how could a poor beggarman turn into a Sea Captain? 'Tisn't possible!"

16
Seven Beggars

rogeen trotted all round the harbour looking at the boats. He longed to go in one but feared he hadn't enough money.

"I wonder now could I do a bit of shoemaking!" he thought.

A fisherman sat in a doorway mending a net.

"Could you tell me is there any chance for a good shoemaker in these parts?" asked the leprechaun.

The fisherman blinked at him for the sun was in his eyes.

"I'm afeard we all mend our own shoes in Cloneytubber and 'tisn't often we treat ourselves to a new pair. But the shoemaker of Knockgobbin across the river has given up his business and gone to foreign parts. You'd earn a mint of money there!"

"How would I get over?" asked Brogeen.

"I've a friend over in Knockgobbin. We'll pull over and see what he's doing with himself. Are you any use in a boat?"

"I wouldn't know," replied the leprechaun humbly. "I've never been in one!"

"God bless me soul!" cried the fisherman.

Without another word he rolled his net and led the way to a bright blue rowing boat. Brogeen stowed his saucepan and his bag in the stern and sat on the middle seat.

"That's where the rower sits," the fisherman told him.

"I'd like to try," said Brogeen. "'Tis terrible good of you to bring me!"

The fisherman slipped the oars into the rowlocks and showed Brogeen how to use them. When the leprechaun started to row, the oars seemed scarcely to touch the water, yet the boat shot out of the harbour away on to the river.

"I never seen a little chap your size row so well!" declared the fisherman.

Brogeen could see fishes swimming from up the river and down the river to catch a sight of him. A seagull dipped slowly, then soared into the sky, screaming, *A leprechaun is on the water! A leprechaun is on the water!* From both shores birds came flocking, so many the fisherman was terrified. Then he saw the fish swarming round the boat.

"Pull in the oars, lad!" he ordered. "Help me get out the net!"

Brogeen wouldn't help to punish the fish for their curiosity.

"Didn't you want to call on your friend?" he asked, sending the boat skimming towards the far shore.

"He's waited twenty years—can't he wait a little longer?" demanded the fisherman. "And why wouldn't he come over to see me?"

Brogeen gave another stroke and the boat touched the bank.

"Is there anything I could do for you?" he asked, stepping on shore.

The fisherman chuckled.

"You've done it! All me life I wanted to meet with a leprechaun. You're a great little rower! Anytime you get tired of the shoemaking send word to Billy Mangan of Cloneytubber, that's me, and he'll find you a job. Now I must be off to me fishing. I never seen so many fish in the river before!"

"Now how did he find out I am a leprechaun?" wondered Brogeen.

As he went towards the town, passengers

from a small river steamer were walking down the gangplank. Last of all came a bent, old man, with a bundle of books under his arm. The books were so big and awkward Brogeen was sorry for him.

"Could I give you a hand with the books?" he asked.

At once the old scholar dumped them into the leprechaun's arms.

Brogeen nearly dropped them. He let go of the saucepan and the apples went rolling along the path. They didn't roll far, for a horde of children, who were kicking a ball, raced after them and by the time Brogeen picked up his saucepan there wasn't an apple to be seen.

"Take better care of the books than you did of the apples," the old man warned him. "I'd be lost without my books!"

"Where will I carry them?" asked Brogeen, walking very slowly.

"Where I can read and think! Don't bother me about where we'll go. A learned man like me shouldn't be bothered with trifles. Take care of those books!"

"Are you very learned?" asked Brogeen. "There do be times when I'd like to be learned meself! Do you know a terrible lot? Do you know all that's in those books?"

"I do indeed! I know English, Irish, French and Latin and if there's any more languages in the world, I know them too! Then there's history and geography, not to mention the mathematics!"

Brogeen wanted to listen. But the heavy books were weighing him down. He wouldn't be able to carry them much farther. His saucepan was once more slipping from under his arm and he stopped to rest his load on a windowsill.

As he glanced down, Brogeen saw the old scholar was wearing a shoe on one foot and a boot on the other. The hair under the top hat was red and bushy and, as he stared, that long solemn face creased into a merry smile.

"I said I'd be seeing you!" chuckled the old scholar.

"A beggarman! Then a sea captain! Now a scholar!" exclaimed Brogeen. "What else can you be?"

The beggarman counted on his fingers—"A wizard, a musician, a ballad singer, a storyteller. But a beggar all the time! Seven beggars rolled into one! You can leave the books!"

The beggarman gazed along the street.

"There's a great eating house along there,

kept by a decent widow woman, Peg Roche. You look famished!"

"If I could do a job of work for her," said the leprechaun anxiously, "I wouldn't mind."

The beggarman roared with laughter.

"If it's work you want—come along! Peg will find you all the work in creation. She's a grand woman and a sensible one. She'd never expect a beggarman to work!"

"Mebbe she wouldn't," thought Brogeen. "But I'm no beggarman. I'm a shoemaker!"

The eating house was a two-roomed cabin. Peg lived in one room with her cat. The other was nearly filled with a table and two long wooden benches. The beggarman stood before the open door and began to sing—

> "Will I sing yez the song
> Of a poor Irish boy,
> Whose life was all sorra,
> Wid no hope of joy.

> "He loved his dear mother
> And his father likewise,
> Till they both died and went
> To their home in the skies.

> "He wept and he sorrad,
>   Until he died too.
> So give me your pity
>   And a bit of help—do!"

People were passing but no one listened, or stopped, or looked.

"They're a hard-hearted set of screws and hucksters!" growled the beggarman. "No thought for anyone but themselves. I must try again.

> "Come listen to me song,
>   For I won't detain yez long.
> Once I was young and full of fire;
>   I'd dance all night and never tire.
> But now I'm growing old—
>   Sure we're all a growing old.
> Oh the days is long and the nights is cold,
>   And we're all a growing old!"

A thin, worried-looking little woman peeped out. When she saw the singer, her worries seemed to drop away from her. She straightened her shoulders and laughed.

"Come along in, ballad singer! We've missed ye this long time in Knockgobbin. There's a bit of pig's cheek and a slab of white cabbage keeping hot, 'twould do you good to look at, let alone eat. Come along in!"

Then she saw Brogeen standing there, not knowing what to do.

"Are you another ballad singer?" she asked sternly. "I couldn't do with two ballad singers!"

"No indeed, ma'am !" replied the leprechaun. "I'm a shoemaker! I heard there was a deal of work to be done in these parts!"

"He's my friend !" cried the beggarman. "I'd share anything I had with Brogeen!"

And he pulled the little shoemaker in with him.

They sat down at the table and the woman brought out a dish of pig's cheek lying on white cabbage. The beggarman cut it in two equal parts. Brogeen took such little bites he had scarcely started on his before the beggarman was finished. So he cut Brogeen's share in two and they started again. Once more the beggarman finished first and once more Brogeen's share was cut in two. This time he ate as fast as he could and when the beggarman looked round, the leprechaun's plate was as clean as his own.

Now they had to squeeze up to the end of the table for the passengers off the steamboat were finding their way to Peg Roche's. She was so busy bringing cups of tea, sandwiches, cuts of bread and butter, she had no time for the beggarman and Brogeen.

"Couldn't we give Peg a hand?" whispered the little shoemaker, who didn't like to see the poor woman working so hard.

His red-haired companion nodded. "I'll do me endeavours," he said grandly.

Peg Roche came in with a loaded tray and the beggarman shook his fingers at it. The cups rose in the air and flew to the table, each settling itself before a customer. The sandwiches and bread and butter followed the tea. Peg nearly dropped the tray.

But the hungry people were only too pleased to be so quickly served.

Unluckily, the beggarman was so delighted with his cleverness, he determined to do better. When Peg came back with the heavy teapot to refill the cups, he sent it round the table to do the job by itself.

Brogeen stood up to watch the pot tilt its spout and pour out the tea. Maybe the beggarman wanted to be sure he had a good drink, but the cups were only half-filled.

"I want a full cup!" grumbled a big man whose hat was pulled down over his eyes.

He held out the cup but the teapot wouldn't stop. The man stared in amazement when he saw the pot going in and out between the people, only half-filling the cups.

Peg tried to grab it. The pot flew over the table out of reach. Some of the customers laughed, others were angry. The man who had complained, clutched the pot by the spout. It poured hot tea over his fingers and he gave the big teapot a shove that sent it with a crash to the floor.

"I'm sorry, ma'am!" he said. "Only 'tisn't right to play tricks on customers!"

Flinging down his money, he marched out into the street.

The other people drank their half-cups of tea and quickly followed him.

"They won't come here again!" said Peg Roche sorrowfully.

"Why wouldn't they?" demanded the beggarman. "Didn't they get a lovely trick given them for nothing with their tea?"

"Tricks is tricks and tay is tay!" declared Peg. "Ye daren't mix them! And there's me grand taypot destroyed on me!"

"Couldn't you do a trick and make it come whole again?" asked Brogeen hopefully, as he watched Peg picking up the pieces.

The beggarman shook his head. "That's a trick beyond my powers!" he sighed.

Then he began to laugh. He laughed so that he had to put his elbows on the table and hold his head. The table shook, the crockery rattled. While he was still laughing, Brogeen followed Peg Roche into the other room.

From his pocket he took a gold piece.

"Would this make up for the teapot that was destroyed?" he asked. "I'm afeard I haven't enough ordinary money to pay for it."

Peg rubbed her eyes.

"Sure, I haven't seen a gold piece in years, not since I was a young one. They don't make them now! Mebbe the schoolmaster, or the doctor, or Father Molony himself will tell me what to do with it!"

"Change it for the biggest teapot you can find!" Brogeen advised her.

He tiptoed out of the cabin while she was still admiring the gold coin and the beggarman's laughter followed him until he had left the last house in Knockgobbin behind.

17

Frightened Fishermen

rogeen walked and walked. The road by the river was busy. A bus went by and Brogeen wondered would he ever journey in such a marvellous carriage. Bicycles, motor cars, carts rattled along. A flock of sheep and a few friendly calves walked at the side.

Yet the leprechaun was lonely. Every time a man passed, even a man riding on a horse, he looked eagerly to see if the stranger had red hair or if he wore one boot and one shoe. He had run away from the beggarman. Now he wished the beggarman would follow him.

"Seven beggars, he told me," thought Brogeen. "I've seen him as a sea captain. I've seen him as a learned scholar. I heard him as a singer and I've seen him doing wizard tricks. All the time he told a good story. But I liked him best as a beggarman down by the river. I never did know him as a musicianer. He'd be powerful with a fiddle or a melodeon."

The road turned inland but Brogeen liked being by the river, so he kept straight on. He came to a tunnel cut in the rock with gaps on the side nearest the water.

Two old men were sitting there among a confusion of nets, lobster pots and flat fish boxes. One was making a net, the other shaped an oar.

"Grand day!" said Brogeen.

The old men didn't answer. Shading their eyes, for the sun was dazzling, they watched half a dozen boats moving into a semi-circle. The leprechaun watched too, for the men in the boats were drawing in their nets.

Brogeen could see the silvery fish leaping and stood up on a rock so that he could see better.

"A fine catch, John James," said one old man.

"I never seen a better, Jer Reardon!" agreed the other.

Suddenly the fishermen let go the nets, the fish leaping and sliding, escaped back to the water.

"What made them do that?" cried Brogeen.

"Didn't they want the fish?"

"You're a stranger!" said John James.

"I've only just come!" explained the leprechaun.

"What can you know of our troubles?" asked Jer Reardon.

"Nothing at all!" answered Brogeen. "But if you are in trouble I'm sorry!"

"Look!" said John James.

With his thin hand he pointed along the shore and the leprechaun saw a long, long man, doubled in two, wading from the water. He was shaking his fists and shouting angrily.

"That's a queer-looking chap!" exclaimed Brogeen. "Queer enough!" agreed the old men.

"What has he to do with the fishermen letting go their catch?" asked the leprechaun impatiently.

"Did you never hear tell of the Pest of Coolgarriv?" asked Jer Reardon.

"I never did!" Brogeen told him.

"When you come to the end of this passage, you'll find our village climbing up the cliff. Once it was the snuggest, happiest village in all Ireland. The fishing was good, every cabin had its patch of land with a few apple trees, a pig, a goat, fowls and some even had a cow."

"Them was the days!" sighed old John

James.

"Then came the Pest!" continued Jer Reardon. "He came at night. Those who first saw him thought he was a shadow, he looked so long and thin. His wife was as thin but not so long. We didn't mind. There was plenty for all."

"He was useful too—at first!" murmured John James.

"At first," agreed Jer Reardon. "He could smell the rain when it was miles away. He could see the wind coming, hours before it came and, better still, he could see the fish when they were out in the ocean. Besides, they lived up in the Giant's Castle beyond the wood, out of the way!"

"We thought they were out of the way!" muttered John James.

The old men nodded at one another. Brogeen was settled comfortably beside them. He wished they would go on with their work. He had learned to row. He would he glad to be able to make a net and shape an oar. But Jer Reardon wanted to tell the troubles of the people of Coolgarriv and John James thought they should be told.

"That long, lean disgrace to the tribe of giants grew tired of telling us fishermen when the fish were coming and taking his share. He'd wait 'til our dinners were cooked then he and his missis would come down and eat the lot. We kept watch and when we'd see them coming, we'd hide the food. They stole our eggs and our hens and now he comes down to meet the fleet when they're bringing in the catch. It isn't only what he takes. He destroys as much as would keep us all in comfort."

" 'Tis shocking to have a hungry giant around," groaned John James. "And we're all hungry too!"

The leprechaun stood up.

"I must be on me way," he said.

"Beware of the Pest!" John James warned him.

"I will!" promised Brogeen.

18

Aideen

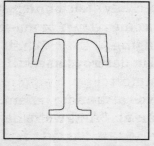he leprechaun came out at the end of the tunnel and took a rocky path which climbed beside the village.

There weren't any people in the street or at the doors, or looking out of the windows. Brogeen would have thought the place deserted only for the thin streams of smoke which came from the chimneys.

There were rocks scattered everywhere. Trees had been pulled up and flung down. Fences were broken and walls overturned. It was such a sad little village Brogeen sighed deeply.

He was growing weary when the path stopped at a pool, covered with purple water-lilies. The path continued on the other side and Brogeen began to walk round at the water's edge. The ground was so marshy his feet became wet, his stockings were soaked and when he sank up to his knees he became almost alarmed.

"I should have kept to the road," he told himself. "All me troubles come from not doing what I should do! Only then I'd never have heard about the Pest."

The broad lily leaf stretched towards him. He scrambled on and it bore him up. Stepping carefully to the next leaf, he leaped for a third and there he was, safe on the path on the other side, while the water-lilies heaved and splashed behind him.

"Whisha, I'm tired!" grumbled the little fellow.

He perched on a rock above the pool, slipped lower so that he could lean back, stretched his legs and took the saucepan from his head.

To his surprise he discovered a cake of soda bread and a piece of soft creamy cheese he had forgotten.

Scarcely had he taken one bite when he heard a scream and a long-legged girl with a cloud of long hair streaming behind her, rushed by.

"I won't go back to Mrs Dominick!" she sobbed. "I won't! I won't!"

As she vanished behind a clump of bushes, a

short stout woman, red and panting, trotted up to Brogeen.

"Which way did she go?" gasped the woman, flopping down beside him.

"Over yonder, ma'am!" replied Brogeen, looking away from the bushes

"I'm no tell-tale!" he thought. "But the poor woman is in a state!"

"Would you like a bit of bread and cheese?" he asked politely. "You'd be very welcome!"

"Thank ye, kindly," she answered. "I'd sooner have a drink of water and I'd give the two eyes out of my head for a sup of tay!"

Brogeen took the saucepan and went down to the pool.

When he returned he stood before the woman, handed her the brimming saucepan and murmured—

"Let it be what herself wants!"

She lifted the saucepan to her lips and nearly dropped it.

"Tay!" she cried. "I haven't tasted tay like that since the fishing went wrong on us be raison of the Pest!"

She drank and drank until the saucepan was empty.

"You're a kind little fella!" she said. "I'll be going home now. If ye do set eyes on Aideen,

that gerrul of mine, tell her to go back to Mrs
Dominick like a good child and not be
annoying me!"

"I will, ma'am!" promised Brogeen. "Will
you take a bite of bread and cheese?"

"I will not then. There's a pot of yalla
turnips boiling on the fire, and a bacon bone to
give them a taste. There's not much
nourishment in turnips but 'tis all we have
now.

The leprechaun shook his head as he turned
once more to his bread and cheese.

"Hallo, mister," said a mournful voice. "I'm
awful hungry!"

Brogeen, his mouth full, looked up.

The girl he had seen running was standing
beside him, her bare legs scratched with
brambles, her face dirty. She wore a short
cotton frock and a long white apron, torn and
crumpled.

"You're Aideen, I suppose?" asked Brogeen,
holding up a piece of bread and cheese.

The girl grabbed it and without a word of
thanks, crammed her mouth and gobbled the
food.

"Haven't you any more?" she asked.

The leprechaun shook his head.

"Anything to drink?"

"Fill the saucepan at the pool and we'll see," said Brogeen crossly.

Aideen tossed her head. The sun caught her brown hair so that it looked like a veil of gold.

"Fill it yourself! I'm not a servant!" she declared scornfully.

Brogeen filled the saucepan with water and, when she tasted it, Aideen discovered it was rich, fresh milk.

"Are you a magician?" she asked respectfully.

The leprechaun did not answer that. Instead he asked a question.

"If you're not a servant, Aideen, what are you?"

Aideen smoothed the tattered apron over her knees and told him proudly—"I'm a princess!"

Brogeen rubbed his nose thoughtfully.

"A princess!" he repeated.

"I suppose you've never met a princess before?" asked the girl, looking at him through the tangled masses of her hair.

"One or two," he murmured. "One or two!"

"What were they like?" Aideen wanted to know.

"Well-mannered, kind-hearted, clean, decent girls, or they wouldn't have been princesses long," declared the leprechaun, folding his arms and looking at her firmly.

"Of course these are my oldest clothes!" said Aideen. "I just put them on for fun. If you saw me in my best clothes, you'd know at once that I'm a princess!"

"'Twouldn't hurt if you washed your face and combed your hair—for a start!" suggested Brogeen, lying back, his legs crossed, his hands clasped behind his head.

"That's no way to sit when you're talking to a princess," grumbled Aideen.

But she washed her face in the pool, dried it on her apron, combed her hair with her fingers and sat back on her heels.

"Why did you run away from Mrs Dominick?" asked Brogeen.

"Because she never left off scolding!" replied Aideen. "I mean, I don't know what you're talking about!"

She stared at him haughtily.

"Was she a terrible scold?" asked Brogeen softly. Aideen flushed. She pressed her lips firmly together and stood up.

"Thank you for the bread and cheese, and the milk," she said politely. "But the next time you meet a princess, don't ask her silly questions."

She walked off through the trees. Brogeen slung his bag over his shoulder, rinsed his saucepan in the pool, dried it with a handful of grass, put it on his head, saw a path and followed it.

Far off he heard crashing and growling.

"Sounds like thunder," muttered the leprechaun. "Only it isn't thunder."

He walked quickly in the direction of the sounds. The path went uphill but his curiosity made him hurry.

"Hi! Magician!" came a cry through the wood. Brogeen grinned.

"Mebbe I am a bit of a magician in me way," he thought. "Only it doesn't always work. Now that young girl should do what her mother wants. Still if Mrs Dominick's a scold, I can't blame Aideen. I don't like being scolded meself."

"Magician! Magician!" came the cry. "Come back! Come back!"

"Mebbe I will after I've found out what's happening yonder," decided Brogeen, and on he marched.

The noise in front ceased, but behind, Brogeen could hear someone panting, dried twigs cracking and a weary voice pleading—

"Wait for me, magician! Wait for me!"

"The poor child!" said Brogreen.

And he waited.

When she came up with him, Aideen looked as untidy as ever. There were leaves and twigs in her hair. She had fallen in a muddy patch and her knees, her apron and her hands were muddy.

"You are in a state!" exclaimed Brogeen.

"Mebbe that Mrs Dominick isn't too much to blame for scolding," he thought.

The girl clutched his arm.

"Don't go that way!" she whispered. "There's a giant lives over there! If you meet him, he'll pick you up and throw you into the air so that you'll never come down again."

"Giant!" scoffed Brogeen. "I'd like to see the giant could catch me!"

But he began to walk in the other direction.

"Speak softly!" Aideen warned him. "You were good to me, so I couldn't let you go into danger. Come quickly! He might hear us. Quiet now. He may have gone away. But you can't be sure. He can move softly, because he's not a real giant. He's only a Pest!"

Brogeen stopped.

"I've never seen a giant!" he muttered. "I'd like to see one if only to tell about, if ever I go back to the Fort, or even the boreen."

"I can show you where he lives," said Aideen. "There's a Look-out beyond the trees. If we climb to the top we can see for miles and miles. And the Pest won't be able to come up on us unbeknownst!"

"I'll come!" agreed the leprechaun. "But I shouldn't be looking for giants. I'm seeking a pair of green shoes!"

"Green shoes!" cried Aideen. "I'd love a pair of green shoes!"

"If only I could come up with them!" said Brogeen. "I made them with me own two hands, so I could go travelling. Well, I'm travelling! But where's me shoes!"

Aideen looked at him wonderingly.

"Are you a shoemaker as well as a magician?" she asked.

"I'm a shoemaker! None better! But what business is it of yours?"

Brogeen looked at her suspiciously. She stared back at his long cap hanging down under the saucepan, his leather apron, the little bag over his shoulder.

Her eyes grew bigger and bigger.

"Are you a—?" she began.

"I don't like questions any more than you do!" snapped Brogeen. "Let's be on our way to this Look-out!"

"Yes, shoemaker!" agreed Aideen meekly. But Brogeen could see she was still wondering.

The path vanished. The ground under the trees was soft bog. Aideen broke a straight branch in two and gave the short piece to the leprechaun. Using it as a leaping pole Brogeen caught up and passed his companion. Soon she was in front again.

"You can't lead! You don't know where we're going!" exclaimed Aideen, as they came out from the twilight of the trees on to a wide paved terrace.

Brogeen leaped beside her, flung away his branch and stood, hands on hips, staring up at a high grey tower, with an open top.

He thought of the Queen's Tower at the Fort of Sheen. "If I climbed up there, I might see her!"

Already Aideen was running up the wide steps which led from the terrace to the base of the tower.

"You'll not run so when you're half-way up," chuckled the leprechaun.

Steep, narrow steps went round and round inside the tower. Aideen clutched the handrail and mounted steadily. She breathed quickly. She began to pant.

"Will I give you a bit of a push or a pull?" asked Brogeen.

"You will not!" answered Aideen ungratefully.

But she let him hold her hand and found herself running up the steps as quickly as if they were going down.

"You are clever!" exclaimed Aideen, as they stood on the flat top of the tower.

"I know as much as the next one!" said Brogeen.

A low parapet guarded the front. They leaned over and gazed across the trees as far as the shore. A small fishing craft was sailing out, its red patched sail looking no bigger than Aideen's apron.

"That's daddy's boat!" said Aideen. "I hope he gets back before the Pest sees him!"

The boat went out of sight before they were tired of looking at it. Aideen showed Brogeen the village where her mother lived.

"And that's the house of horrid Mrs Dominick!" she added.

Brogeen didn't say a word. Aideen tried to look at him without turning her head. Her face grew redder and redder.

"I wonder how a princess comes to have a fisherman for a father and to be in dread of poor Mrs Dominick?" murmured the leprechaun.

"Couldn't I be lost and found on a doorstep?" asked Aideen indignantly.

"Mebbe you could," agreed Brogeen. But he was grinning.

"I won't stay here to be insulted!" exclaimed Aideen.

"I'd like to set eyes on that selfsame giant!" jeered Brogeen.

"You have your wish!" roared a terrible voice.

A huge hand snatched Brogeen from one side of the tower and Aideen from the other!

19

The Pest

"P on me word!" exclaimed Brogeen furiously. "Creeping up behind!"

"Put me down! Put me down!" screamed Aideen.

They became silent as they were twisted round and looked upon a pair of huge eyes, a monster nose and a great grinning mouth with teeth like milestones.

"So you're the Pest!" said the leprechaun at last.

"I'm the Pest!" chuckled the horrible creature.

Though no thicker than an ordinary man, he was as tall as the tower and his first finger and thumb went easily about the girl and the leprechaun.

"Put me down and I won't tell anyone!" pleaded Aideen. At once the great fingers opened and down they fell, whirling and twisting until they reached the ground. Luckily they didn't land on the terrace but on the soft ground beyond. Yet they were so shaken and bruised they lay still, fearful and trembling.

"It would be fun to throw ye up in the air for a mile or more!" exclaimed the giant. "That'd larn ye! Only I'm too kind! I'll hand ye over to the missis, to clean, the pots and scrub the floor, and find something for us to eat."

Brogeen stood up, shaky but defiant.

"You daren't do that to a princess!" he said.

"Ho! Ho! Ho!" roared the giant. "That one a princess! She's a quare princess! Look at her!"

"A princess could be disguised!" said the leprechaun.

The Pest wasn't convinced but he didn't disbelieve.

"Princess she may be but the missis needs help in the kitchen. I'll bring the two of you along. If she says so ye can stay and earn your keep. If she won't have you, I'd be sorry for what's left when I've finished with ye!"

"The impudence of that one!" muttered Brogeen.

The saucepan was over his eyes, so that he couldn't see. He pulled it off and gave a jump.

Brogeen and the Green Shoes

It wasn't much of a jump for he was bruised and tired. But before he began to come down, he jumped a bit more and kept on jumping until he was on a level with the top of the Look-out and found himself staring into the Pest's eyes.

The Pest was furious but puzzled. He didn't understand the strange pair he had captured. Brogeen gave his last jump and the Pest blinked as the leprechaun, raising the saucepan with both hands, gave the big red nose so close to him a tremendous whack!

"Oh!" roared the Pest and the wind of his breath sent the leprechaun tumbling on to the Look-out.

Brogeen didn't know it but the Pest's nose was his weakest spot. He rubbed and roared, his eyes shut, his great hands reaching our for the leprechaun.

"I'd best get away from this shocking place!" thought Brogeen. "Now's me chance!"

Only there was Aideen lying on the ground, looking up at him, her face pale, her eyes frightened.

"If she wasn't so heavy," muttered the little fellow, "I'd get away safe with her."

"Me poor boy!" said a strange voice. "What ails ye?"

"A spiteful midget beat me on the nose!" blubbered the Pest. "Oh, the pain of it! Catch him! Catch him!"

"The great bully!" said the stranger. "Where is he?"

Brogeen peeped over the edge of the Lookout. A thin woman was standing beside the Pest, shaking her head. She didn't seem really concerned. She was very thin and didn't reach much higher than the Pest's waist. For all that she was taller than most people.

"Did you beat the poor fella?" she asked Aideen.

More terrified than ever, the girl shook her head.

Brogeen leaned out as far as he could.

"'Twas the Pest started it!" Aideen was saying, when the leprechaun reached the ground.

"Saucy hussy!" exclaimed the woman. "How dare you call my husband the Pest!"

The Pest was still feeling his nose tenderly.

"I'll shut them in the dungeon!" he growled. "I'll beat them black and blue! They can help you in the kitchen, Moggie!"

"If they're going to help me in the kitchen, you can't shut them in the dungeon!" declared Moggie. "I'll be glad of their company. Nobody seems to like us in these parts!"

"What do you expect?" cried Aideen indignantly. "You've destroyed the fishing, pulled up our apple trees, broken our fences. You should be ashamed!"

"So you should!" agreed the leprechaun.

He admired Aideen's courage though he thought her very rash to provoke the Pest. But the great creature wasn't listening and Moggie didn't mind.

"Don't blame him!" she said. "He's just a big, light-hearted boy! He really wants everyone to be happy, only he's always misunderstood."

She led the way. Aideen walked with Brogeen and the Pest came last, stumbling because he wouldn't bother to notice where he was stepping.

"If 'twasn't for his size, he'd be nothing to be afraid of," thought the leprechaun. "He's shocking big!"

Before them, on the bare mountain side, was a castle built of huge blocks of stones. Most of it was in ruins but from one chimney flared a banner of smoke.

"You'll have to help with the housework," said Moggie. "You won't mind that, will you? All nice girls like housework."

"I'm a princess!" declared Aideen haughtily.

"A princess doesn't do housework!"

The woman laughed until she choked. The leprechaun leaped up and thumped her on the back.

"A princess!" she spluttered. "If that one's a princess, I'm an empress! The little fella's a king!"

Brogeen was almost as angry as Aideen.

"I'm a shoemaker!" he declared. "I'm the best shoemaker in Ireland, and if it wasn't for a bit of trouble I've had with a pair of green shoes, you'd not have set eyes on me!"

"Never mind me," said the woman consolingly. "I like a joke! Keep on walking!"

The Pest, impatient at the delay, stepped over them and strode up to the castle. There was no door so he went straight in and the others followed.

20

Apple Dumplings

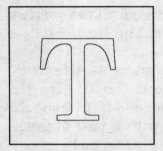hey came into a long room. There were holes in the walls but no windows. At one side a log fire smouldered. A slab of rock lay in the middle of the room and served as a table. There were square stones against the wall. These were the chairs.

"What a horrid, dirty place!" exclaimed Aideen, wrinkling her nose.

"If that's what you think," retorted Moggie, "you can start cleaning up!"

"Couldn't we take the crocks out to the stream?" suggested Brogeen, who was almost as shocked as Aideen.

"Have you a tray?" asked the girl.

Moggie laughed.

"Aren't you very particular! Take them in your apron and don't pretend, Princess!"

Aideen frowned.

"My father calls me Princess, and he should know!" she declared.

The Pest sat at the table sideways, his legs stretched out.

Aideen, Moggie and the leprechaun carried the dishes and pans to the stream.

"That's a lovely colour!" said the leprechaun. "'Tis like the feast wine we drank in the Fort."

He filled his saucepan and sipped then let the lovely drink trickle faster and faster down his dry throat.

"I never tasted better water, not ever!" he declared.

The woman laughed.

"Ye foolish little fella! That's not water!" she told him.

"What is it then?"

"Cider!"

Brogeen rubbed his chin.

"Isn't cider made from apples?"

"Of course it is! Every omadhaun knows that!"

The leprechaun was annoyed.

"There's no manners in this place!" he said sharply.

The woman looked down at Brogeen, smiling.

"Sure, I didn't mean to vex ye! We're very uncultivated up here. There's times I'm sorry I didn't stay where I belonged. I thought 'twould be grand to marry a giant and live in a castle! How could I know?"

"Can't you do something about it!" asked Brogeen sympathetically.

"What can I do?"

"Dinner!" came a roar from the castle.

"Hark at him!" said Moggie. "That's the way he always is. Thinks of nothing but eating!"

"I could do with a bit of dinner meself," murmured the leprechaun.

"I'm starving!" sighed Aideen.

They trooped into the castle, carrying the crocks and pans, a bit sticky but clean.

"What are ye giving me for me dinner?" demanded the Pest.

"There's a grand pot of praties, nearly boiled!" answered his wife.

"Praties!" roared the Pest. "I'm sick and tired of praties! I want fish! I want meat! I'm famished!"

The tall thin woman marched over to the table.

"'Tis your own fault!" she said. "Who took all the fishermen's catch until 'twasn't a haporth of good them going out? Who stole every bullock for miles around, so that the farmers never had a chance? Tell me that! And the fowls and ducks and everything you could lay your greedy, wasteful hands on!"

The Pest looked serious.

"How was I to know what a spiteful, vindictive set of people live here!" he demanded. "They're ungrateful too! While I'm living in this castle, they're safe. If they drive me away with their tantrums, who knows what might happen to them?"

"They wouldn't mind taking a chance!" jeered Moggie. "Where else can we go? At least we have a roof over our heads and we can still steal a bit to eat!"

"Bread and potatoes!" groaned the Pest. "There's no nourishment in them, and the bread's always stale!"

He looked so mournful Brogeen was sorry for him.

"What have ye in the place at all?" he asked.

The thin woman screwed up her face and thought.

"There's a sack of flour. There's dozens of apples on the trees himself pulled up from the orchards, and that's all!"

"I love apple dumplings!" said Aideen. "Me mammy always bakes apple dumplings on

Friday."

The Pest leaned across the table.

"Can you make apple dumplings?" he asked, his greedy eyes gleaming.

Aideen pouted. Brogeen gave her a poke.

"Of course you can!" he whispered. "A princess must do something."

"I'll try!" said the girl doubtfully.

"I'll have the stove ready!" promised Moggie.

"Hurry up!" ordered the Pest. "I'll want the dumplings as soon as I've finished the praties."

"Here's the flour!" and the thin woman showed Aideen a sack in the corner.

"There's the apples!"

She trotted to a door at the back, flung it open and pointed to a great heap of apple trees. Their withered roots stuck up in the air while apples continually dropped, and fell into the pool below. There they swirled, round and round, crushed and bruised, while the thick juice fermented and mixed with the water.

"So that's how cider is made!" muttered Brogeen.

"Of course there shouldn't be any water!" explained Moggie. "It makes the cider weak and gives a shocking taste to the tea. But what can a poor woman do?"

The leprechaun and Aideen filled a basket with apples and went back to the castle.

"Me mammy always peels and cores the apples," sighed Aideen. "It takes a terrible long time!"

"Then we won't do it!" declared Brogeen.

"Where can we mix the dough?" Aideen asked the woman.

"In the trough, pet! In the trough!"

Moggie helped them tip out the flour. They ran backwards and forwards with saucepans of apple water. Then with three broom handles they stirred and stirred.

"Does your mammy boil or bake the dumplings?" asked Brogeen.

"Sometimes she boils and sometimes she bakes!" Aideen told him. "Baking is quicker!"

"Then we'll bake!" decided Moggie. "The oven's roasting!"

They thumped out pieces of dough and wrapped them round the apples. The apples were big and each one made a good-sized dumpling.

They made twelve and when they were in the oven, Moggie, Aideen, and the leprechaun sat side by side and watched the giant eating.

"Could you do with a pratie?" asked the

Pest's wife.

"I could!" replied Brogeen and Aideen together.

The Pest sat with the cauldron on the table in front of him. It had been full. Now he had to dip down to the bottom.

Moggie reached over and grabbed at the potatoes.

"Put them back, you robber!" ordered the Pest.

"We'll get no nourishment watching you eat!" snapped the thin woman.

She gave one potato to Brogeen, one to Aideen, and ate the rest herself.

A lovely smell crept through the castle.

"Apple dumplings!" murmured Moggie, smiling. "I haven't eaten an apple dumpling since I left home! I'm no great hand at the cooking."

Aideen looked worried.

"I'm not good at cooking either!" she whispered. "I only help me mammy, not often, and Mrs Dominick never makes apple dumplings!"

"More fool she!" declared Moggie. "I wonder if they're cooked!"

She opened the oven door.

"I've just remembered!" exclaimed Aideen.

"What's wrong?" asked Brogeen, softly.

"There should be butter, or lard, or dripping. I forget which! And sugar! I'm afraid they'll be heavy! What will I do?"

"Nothing!" Brogeen told her. "That boyo won't know heavy from light. If he grumbles, let on the oven wasn't hot enough. Say the flour was damp! Tell him the next lot will be grand. Sure, Aideen, they look fine!"

Side by side they went slowly towards the oven. The Pest swung round and peered over his wife's shoulder. Aideen and the leprechaun squeezed beside him.

Twelve apple dumplings lay on the shelf. They were a deep golden brown and the smell of the hot apples was so delicious, Brogeen's mouth watered.

"They look gorgeous! They smell gorgeous!" he said.

The Pest's wife took out four dumplings and placed them on the stone table. The Pest broke his in two, so that it would cool quicker. The apple was like jelly and he began to scrape it out with a big iron spoon.

Aideen leaned across the table.

"I'm afraid the crust's a bit hard and thick," she said, humbly.

"I like it hard and thick!" the Pest grinned

happily.

Brogeen tried to break his dumpling but he couldn't. Neither could Aideen. Moggie beat hers against the edge of the table but the crust would not break. She brought over a knife with a sharp point and split bits off. When at last she uncovered the apple, she ate that.

"That's shocking hard crust!" she muttered. "But the apples are grand, quite sweet!"

"Is them the kind of apple dumplings yer mammy makes?" Moggie asked Aideen.

The girl shook her head.

"Mammy's are light and flaky. My mammy's a lovely cook and I'm so hungry!"

"Here's the knife! Chip your way through!" said the thin woman kindly.

While they were chipping at their dumplings, the Pest had eaten his, crunching up the crust and smacking his lips. He took two more from the oven and kept on eating. While the others were still spooning out the soft apple, he finished the last dumpling.

"You can have my crust," said his wife, pushing it over.

"I can't eat any more but I'd hate to see such good food go to waste!" declared Brogeen, and over went his crust.

Without a word Aideen added her crust to

the heap. The Pest grinned and gobbled happily.

"You can stay here," he said. "You're a wonderful little cook!"

"We'll keep the small fella too," said the Pest's wife. "Even then 'tis a terrible big place to manage if 'tis run as it should be."

"I'm not complaining!" said the Pest, shifting against the wall and leaning back. "I'm that comfortable and contented I could do with a nap."

Brogeen pushed Aideen forward.

"Speak up!" he said. "Remember you're a princess! Stand by your rights and your people's rights!"

"We'd want wages!" declared Aideen desperately. "And you'd have to stop stealing all the fish and pulling up trees and frightening people. If you do that me mammy might come up and lend a hand. I couldn't say for sure but she might!"

The Pest didn't answer. His eyes closed, his mouth fell open, showing great teeth, and he snored.

"I never did like giants!" muttered Brogeen. "They're too big and they have no cultivation!"

"Mind your manners!" snapped the Pest's wife. "Remember 'tis his house you're in!"

"He has no right to it!" declared Aideen, braver and braver now that the Pest was asleep. "And I'm going home!"

The thin woman stared.

"You'll come back," she pleaded. "Bring your mother. I've been so lonely. Tell her if she can keep himself well-fed, there'll be no more bother. Besides he's useful. He can lift rocks, carry loads, dig drains. He's wonderful. That lad could build a ball alley if he put his mind to it. Think what that would do for a village! If the fishermen give him a share of the fish, I'll see he acts right by them. Tell your father that!"

Aideen slipped through the doorway.

"Hi, there!" called the Pest's wife. "If your father's a fisherman and your mother's a fisherman's wife, how can you be a princess?"

"You'll be seeing her! She'll tell you then!" promised the leprechaun.

They went back towards the Look-out. Aideen led the way. She ran. She danced. Brogeen didn't trouble to keep up with her. She stopped again and again, running back, running on, talking all the time.

"I won't have to go back to Mrs Dominick! I'll come up to the castle every day and the boys will come too. When you find your green shoes, will you let me wear them?"

"Wait until I find them!"

"Where do you come from?"

"The Fort of Sheen!"

"Where are you going?"

"The way the green shoes went!"

Brogeen was dropping back. He moved sideways among the trees and every time he answered, his voice sounded fainter.

Aideen went on asking questions without listening for an answer. She was thinking how she had conquered the Pest. Her father could go out fishing. They would all have plenty to eat. No one would be frightened any more. Even if she weren't a princess, she would be in and out of the castle, and she'd never have to go back to Mrs Dominick! Never!

21

Elder-tree Island

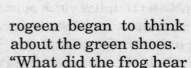rogeen began to think about the green shoes.

"What did the frog hear the big owl say—when Brogeen of the Stepping Stones meets with the Speckled Horse of Waterford, the Pig Cart of Dungarvan and the Shadow Pedlar, on the same day, he's caught up on the green shoes."

"Now where would I meet with all of them?" the leprechaun asked himself.

He stopped to talk to a red cow looking over a fence and then he saw a barge tied to a crumbling, moss-grown post sticking out from the bank—a barge which had been there so long it had grown green as the grass.

"Go along with you!" said the cow. "If it's travelling you're after, now's your chance!"

Brogeen was glad to step on board and sit down. A steamer chugged by and the surge from its passing reached the barge.

The rope, which was nearly as old as the post, snapped. And away went the barge and Brogeen with it.

The sun was high, the wind had dropped. Birds perched on the barge and fishes swam after it.

At first the barge kept close to the shore, poking in among the rushes, turning, twisting and, at last, caught by the tide, swinging out to the middle of the river.

"Mebbe I'll go as far as the salt sea the beggarman told me about when he was a captain," murmured Brogeen, talking to himself for company's sake. "I wonder how much he really knew about the sea, seeing all the time he was only a beggarman?"

"Why wouldn't a beggarman know?" the leprechaun asked a gull that swooped down and perched on the side of the barge. "Doesn't a beggarman travel and see the world more than most of us?"

The gull rattled its bill and looked at Brogeen with its head on one side.

"True for ye," said the leprechaun. "There's good beggarmen and there's bad beggarmen. I don't know why, but I'd sooner be a shoemaker. Mebbe 'tis because I am one!"

The gull screamed and flew away.

"No manners!" declared Brogeen severely. "No manners at all! Now the beggarman had lovely manners, so he had!"

Where an island rose from the water, the barge drifted right into a tiny cove, just large enough to hold it. Elder trees grew down to the water's edge, their branches white with big circles of blossom. The barge bobbed through and came to rest, hidden from boats going up or coming down the river.

The scent of elder flowers, the green shade and the golden light on the water outside made Brogeen drowsy.

He slept and dreamed. In his dreams he followed the green shoes, always a little behind, never catching up. Everywhere he went, the beggarman went with him.

They climbed round the side of the mountain above the boreen. They came to the greenest meadow he had ever seen. The grass was fine and soft but not a flower grew in it. The dog daisies, forget-me-nots, poppies, cornflowers were gathered in a wide band at the edge of the field, they had not ventured into the grass.

Suddenly a piece of the meadow reared up. The beggarman turned and ran, calling

Brogeen to follow him. The leprechaun, though terrified, stood still. The piece of the meadow came slowly towards him and Brogeen saw it was a cow, a green cow, so green, no wonder he had thought it part of the field.

"I've met red cows, and black ones, and white ones, and I've met cows with red and black patches, but you're the first green cow that's come my way!" exclaimed Brogeen.

The cow waved its tail and went on chewing thoughtfully. "I don't suppose you'll meet another," she said proudly. "I'm very special!"

"Why are you green?" asked Brogeen.

The cow chewed and chewed.

"Because I'm contented!" she answered.

"Sure, you're not the only one that's contented!" objected the leprechaun. "Yet the others aren't green!"

The cow stopped chewing.

"Mebbe they didn't eat grass!" she said.

"All the cows I ever knew ate grass!" Brogeen told her. "Why weren't they green?"

"Because they weren't contented, of course!" she said kindly. "Now is there anything else you want to know?"

The leprechaun tiptoed close to her.

"Would the green shoes he hiding here?" he

whispered.

The cow switched her tail.

"I'm not the Speckled Horse of Waterford. I'm not the Pig Cart of Dungarvan. I'm not the Shadow Pedlar. So why should you think you've come up with the green shoes?"

"True enough!" said Brogeen sadly. "True enough!"

The green cow walked away, mooing. "Keep on, Brogeen! Keep on!"

Then he was home again in his house under the beech. The days were long and hot, the sun shone, he went visiting and saw all his friends.

While Brogeen slept, the sun shone steadily through the elder branches, at night the moon rose full and clear. Time passed and still he dreamed.

The leaves began to fall and Brogeen woke. The elder flowers had gone and the berries were forming. As he watched they changed from green to red, from red to black.

"That was a powerful long sleep!" said Brogeen. "I don't know when I enjoyed a rest more."

He sat up. His clothes were ragged, his shoes worn thin. He was terribly hungry.

"Them was grand dreams!" he murmured.

But were they dreams? The leprechaun couldn't be sure.

He gave a push at the trunk of an elder tree. Out from its hiding place drifted the barge, down the river which grew wider and wider.

Brogeen had never seen so many boats before. Some darted along like dragonflies. Others, heavily laden, went about their business. Some towered like fortresses, many were smaller than the barge.

Brogeen felt his feet cold and wet. The old rotten planks were giving way and he had to sit up on the side to keep dry.

"I'm afeard I'll have to swim for it," grumbled the leprechaun, feeling small and frightened, and terribly sorry for himself.

The bank was still distant. A steamer, pointing down the river, churned up strong, foaming waves. One caught the barge, twisting it round and giving it a thrust towards a jetty. Holding tight to his bag and his saucepan, Brogeen leaped through the air and landed safely, as the barge sank quietly to the bottom.

Brogeen found it hard to walk properly after being on the barge for so long. The planks of the quay where he found himself rose to meet him. The shops on the far side swayed and danced. He leaned against a barrel with his back to the river and gazed at the houses climbing the hill.

A smell of cakes and hot bread drew Brogeen across the road to a shop with a big glass window filled with tarts. Farther on was another cake shop even better than the first. But it was so grand the little shoemaker was afraid to go inside. Round the next corner he found a cake shop so small and dark the customers had to grope their way to the counter and feel their way back to the street.

"'Tis no way at all to have a shop," thought Brogeen indignantly. "But for all that there's a lovely smell coming out of it."

He went from cake shop to bakery, from bakery to pastry-cook, climbing higher and higher through the town.

"When I've seen all the cake shops there are, mebbe I'll find one where I can have a sup of hot tay. Whish! I never knew there were so many cakes in the world. I might have two with me tea!"

22

Bold Anne

hile Brogeen was floating down the river the green shoes were still roaming through the streets, going farther and farther away from the cobbler's.

They grew tired of the rough roadway, for they had to keep on jumping, so when they found a street with wide paving stones, they followed it uphill, along by a wind-swept market-place to a narrow lane at the top. They kept on to the last house, then they could go no further. They had come to the end of the street and the top of the town.

Far below them Brogeen was going from cake-shop to cake-shop, for the shoemaker and his shoes had come to the same town.

The green shoes rested beside three steps which led to a green door. The house was very small, with a peaked green-tiled roof. The windows were round and flowers grew in boxes on all the windowsills.

The door was open. First a little girl came out. She hopped down the steps, one at a time.

"Wait for me, Anne! Wait for me!" called a voice.

"I won't wait!" said Anne.

"Don't be bold!" called another voice. "Wait for Patcheen, there's the girl!"

"I won't wait!" whispered Anne.

But she stopped at the foot of the three steps until a boy, even smaller and fatter than Anne, came out.

"You can't hop down the steps one at a time, Patcheen!" she told him.

"I can do everything!" replied the small boy.

He tried to jump the three steps all at once, slipped on the second and sat down on the pavement. He didn't cry but screwed up his mouth and his face became very red.

"I will do it!" declared Patcheen, scrambling up.

Back he went. This time he took the steps in three jumps. "Did it!" he said, put his hand in Anne's and away they went.

"You must keep in step with me," Anne told him. "Left, right! Left, right!"

When the green shoes heard this, they

marched along too, Left beside Patcheen, Right beside Anne.

"Both together!" said Anne.

"Both together!" repeated Patcheen.

Anne was speaking to her brother. He spoke to the green shoe, trying to keep in step with him. Patcheen didn't know how unusual it was for shoes to be walking about by themselves. But when Anne looked down and saw Right squeezing along the kerb beside her, she was startled.

"Where are we going?" asked Patcheen.

"To the toffee shop!" replied Anne, looking away from the shoes for a moment.

When she looked again they weren't there. But a little man with a long cap, bag over his shoulder and a bright saucepan under his arm, was standing beside her.

"That's a shocking road to cross!" he said to her.

"Keep with us!" Anne told him. "We're going over to the toffee shop."

"You're very kind!" said Brogeen.

"Don't run and keep together!" ordered Anne.

She clutched Patcheen's hand. He hated crossing roads but when they were half-way over, he looked round for the green shoes.

"They've run away!" he grumbled. "I liked those green shoes. I'm going back to look for them!"

Anne tightened her grip and they reached the toffee shop safely.

"You wait here for us!" Anne told the leprechaun.

He stood on tiptoe to look in at the window. It was filled with toffee, from plain brown toffee in flat tins to square blocks of Everton toffee, set proudly in the middle. Beyond, Brogeen could see Anne standing at the counter.

Brogeen had never seen a little girl he liked better. She had a dimple in her chin and one on each cheek. There were dimples on her knees and her wrists. Where other people had knuckles, she had dimples, and when she came out of the shop, she was carrying a big toffee apple on a stick.

She held out the apple to the leprechaun. "You can have first bite!" she told him.

She gave Patcheen a bite and had one herself. They kept on, turn by turn, and it was lucky the apple was a big one.

"What's your name?" Anne asked the little shoemaker.

"I'm Brogeen—Brogeen of the Stepping Stones!" he told her.

"I've always wanted to meet a leprechaun, ever since I was as small as Patcheen!" she said, biting the apple.

Brogeen stared.

"How do you know I'm a leprechaun?" he asked in amazement.

"Sure, everybody knows what a leprechaun looks like! I expect the green shoes we met belong to you!"

"They do! They do!" cried Brogeen. "They ran away from me and I'm follying them! I was told I'm never catch up with them, till I meet the Speckled Horse of Waterford, the Pig Cart of Dungarvan and the Shadow Pedlar, on the one day. That doesn't seem possible and I'm thinking I'd better have stayed in the boreen until they grew tired of wandering and came home."

Anne gave him another bite.

"We'll help you!" she promised. "Won't we, Patcheen?"

Patcheen nodded. Already he had toffee on his nose and chin, and there were bits even on his curly hair. Anne managed the apple a little better, but her face and hands were so sticky it was a wonder there was any toffee to eat.

They strolled along, keeping step. Brogeen was feeling happier. Anne nudged him.

"There's the Speckled Horse of Waterford!" she said, pointing.

The leprechaun looked up. A black and white horse, standing in a gateway, gazed down the street towards the river. Patcheen slapped the horse's leg with his sticky hand but it didn't move.

"It waits there all day long," explained Anne. "When the moon shines down the street, it gallops away over the water!"

"Can you beat that!" murmured Brogeen.

He was very sticky but he didn't mind anything now.

"'Twas the lonesomeness troubling me," he thought. "'Tis terrible to be alone and lost, and away from home!"

He smiled at Anne. She smiled back.

"This is me second best frock," she said. "So I mustn't wipe me hands on it! What shall I do?"

Brogeen didn't know.

"Lick them, like me!" Patcheen told her.

They walked on, licking their fingers and, though Anne did her best, the frock was soon as sticky as her face and her brown hair was glistening.

"Pig Cart!" said Patcheen, his mouth still full of toffee apple.

The cart was coming down from the market. Brogeen couldn't see what was in it, for it passed in a flash.

"Of Dungarvan?" asked Brogeen.

Anne nodded. "Of course!" she replied.

They had finished the outside covering of toffee and the sour juicy apple made them feel less sticky and uncomfortable. But Brogeen wondered if he would ever again drink a cup of hot tea. "You wouldn't know where I'd find the Shadow Pedlar?" he asked.

"Me Auntie Maggie will tell you that! She knows everything!" cried Anne. "There she is! She's coming to buy me new shoes!"

Aunt Maggie carried a basket in one hand and a market-bag in the other. They were both crowded with parcels wrapped in all kinds of paper and tied with coloured tape. Brogeen wished he knew what was in them.

"Oh, Anne!" exclaimed Aunt Maggie. "You've been eating toffee apples again!"

She turned to Brogeen.

"You should know better!" she scolded. "I'm surprised at you!"

She stopped as a man standing in the gutter began to sing—

"Have you met the Shadow Pedlar
     On your way?
When the moon is shining
     And the day
Has flown away,
     Has flown away.

"If you meet the Shadow Pedlar
     As you run,
When the sun is rising
     Day's begun,
And night is done,
     And night is done."

"That's him!" screamed Anne.

"That's him!" shouted Patcheen, dancing up and down.

The man stopped singing and stood laughing at them.

Brogeen stared. The man had red hair. He wore one shoe and one boot. But when the leprechaun stepped towards him, he darted up a narrow turning filled with shadows, and vanished.

"Never mind! You keep with us!" Anne told Brogeen.

"Here's the boot shop!" said Auntie Maggie. "You need a nice strong pair of boots, Anne!"

"I want green shoes!" declared Anne.

"Don't be bold!" cried her aunt. "Wouldn't I buy you green shoes if they were made? Thanks be they're not!"

They went into the shop. Brogeen followed. There were so many boots and shoes, it was hard to believe anyone in the world could be barefoot.

"There's not one pair to come up to my green shoes!" boasted the leprechaun.

As he spoke the green shoes trotted into the shop. They hopped on a box and from that jumped to the counter.

"What's the meaning of this?" asked the shopman, staring.

"Sure, I'm in the trade!" explained the leprechaun, showing his tools.

"They're the shoes I want!" said Anne.

"Runaways!" murmured Brogeen, but he stroked them, for he couldn't be angry now he had found the shoes.

"They're dancing shoes!" objected Aunt Maggie. But she was just as delighted as Anne.

"If I had them," said Anne, "I'd be the best dancer in the school. I'd be the best in all Waterford. They're the loveliest shoes I've ever seen!"

"Don't be bold now!" said her aunt. "Where would I find the money to pay for shoes like them?"

"If they fit the child, let her have them," said Brogeen. "I made them to be me own travelling shoes. But I've had all the travelling I want. I see now they really are dancing shoes. Try them on, Bold Anne! There's no money can buy them shoes. They're a gift!"

"I'm not always bold!" Anne told him. "Are you sure you want to give me your lovely shoes?"

"I'd sooner you had them than anyone I've ever known!" declared Brogeen. "Didn't you share your toffee apple with me? 'Twas a grand toffee apple!"

The shopman pulled forward a chair.

"I never thought I'd be making a bargain for someone else's shoes," he said, for he didn't understand about not paying for them, "But we live and learn!"

He took off Anne's muddy strap shoes and slipped on the green shoes. They fitted as if the leprechaun had made them specially for her.

Brogeen brought out the glittering buckles Peter the Pedlar had given him. He laid them on the shoes and they stuck fast.

Anne stood up and began to dance.

She danced down the shop and out into the street. Aunt Maggie and Patcheen ran after her. The shop man stood in the doorway. The people in the street began to clap. They could hear her singing—

"I'll dance, and I'll dance, and I'll dance down the street,

With Brogeen the Leprechaun's shoes on me feet!"

"She's a lovely little dancer!" said the shopman. "And the lad that made those shoes is a shoemaker I'd like to meet!"

He turned to speak to Brogeen. But Brogeen was no longer there!

23

The Road Home

rogeen was on his way
home!

"If I keep on and never
turn to the right or the left, I'm bound to get
there!" he decided. "Isn't that what the onion
woman said?"

So he tried to go back the way he had come.

He went down the hill past the Speckled
Horse, along the street to the quay. There he
came to a stop.

"The barge is sunk on me," he grumbled. "So
I can bid goodbye to the river!"

"Hi! Hi!" came a shout from behind him.
"Are ye wanting a job?"

The leprechaun looked over his shoulder
and there was the Pig Cart of Dungarvan.

The man stood by the horse's head looking
very worried.

"Hi!" he called again. "Would ye hold this

horse while I go for a bite and sup? I'm famished!"

He put the reins in Brogeen's hands.

"Don't budge and I'll give ye a whole twopenny bit when I come back," he promised.

Brogeen stared at the horse.

"Get up on me back !" it said.

"Aren't you the Speckled Horse of Waterford?" demanded the leprechaun.

"I am! I am!" neighed the horse impatiently. "And 'tisn't for many I'd be leaving me post in the daytime. Get up!"

"The man expects me to mind his cart," objected Brogeen. "I wouldn't want to be doing him a bad turn. He promised me a twopenny piece and I'd as well have a bite and sup meself before I set off. There's not too much nourishment in a few bites of toffee apple!"

"Sure the Seventh Pig is here, willing and able to take charge," explained the Speckled Horse. "He'll stay till I come back!"

There was a net over the cart. Underneath it a tiny bonaveen lay stretched on clean straw. Now it stood up, pushed back the net, put its front trotters on the seat and squealed pleasantly at Brogeen.

It was quite black and had a blue ribbon tied in a big bow round its neck.

"Will I be doing right?" asked Brogeen anxiously.

"What a leprechaun!" neighed the horse. "He'd take the word of a strange pig before mine."

"Better start!" said a voice Brogeen knew well. "When the setting sun shines on the clock tower 'twill be too late!"

The beggarman strolled over.

"Up with you, Brogeen!" he said.

And there was the leprechaun on the horse's back, his tools and his saucepan before him.

"Take a grip of the mane!" advised the beggarman. "That lad travels fast."

"I was afeard I'd never see you again!" said Brogeen. "Be off!" cried the beggarman's warning voice. The Speckled Horse shook himself free of the harness and swung round as the clock tower face glowed with sunlight. Brogeen looked back.

"Are you the beggarman, or the Shadow Pedlar?" he called.

From the shadows lengthening across the quay came a laugh and then Brogeen heard — "I'll be seeing you! Safe home!"

The Speckled Horse galloped. His hooves thudded on the wooden planks. A great motor bus thundered by. The horse stretched its legs and skimmed the earth so that Brogeen wondered if the long mane streaming on the wind was changing to wings. The lights came out in the bus and they left it behind.

When the road grew quite dark, the Speckled Horse leapt the wall and went straight across a stretch of bog. Some light yet lingered in the golden brown pools but the air was blowing keen.

Brogeen saw stars reflected in a stream and once they jumped over the moon.

They passed through a town where a man was putting up the shutters to a shoe shop.

"I know this place!" said the leprechaun.

They came to a crossroads and at the front of a great hay-cart Carmel, who had given Brogeen the wooden cup, was riding home with her father. She lay against him sound asleep.

The Speckled Horse stopped suddenly at a long low bridge with seven arches.

"I may come no further!" he neighed, lowering his head and bending his knees, so that Brogeen slid easily to the ground.

Before the leprechaun could thank him, he was only a shadow speeding along the road.

Brogeen shivered.

"Whisha, I wonder what will me little house

be like after all this time," he thought, as he trudged across the bridge.

He stumbled out on the road. The moon showed every stone, frost silvered the ruts and crackled beneath his feet.

The wind ran whispering in and out the bushes, along the stone walls, "Here he is! Here he is!"

And there was the phouka, looking one moment like a handsome young pony, the next like a shaggy billy-goat.

Brogeen gave a jump towards the wall to hide himself. Then came back and stood in the middle of the road. He was ashamed of his fear. Wasn't the phouka a friend?

"On me back!" ordered the phouka.

So Brogeen rode to the boreen in style.

"There's some have been before us!" declared the phouka.

Propped against the blackthorn bush was a little wheel-barrow, painted bright blue. One on each side sat Jim and Judy MacDonald, sleepy and shivering.

"Welcome home, Brogeen!" said Judy. "Me mother sent you a few bits of things."

"I made the wheelbarrow," said Jim. "I hope you'll like it!" Brogeen stared, too surprised even to say "Thank you!" "If you sit beside the parcels you could ride home," suggested Judy. "You must be terribly tired! Peter the Pedlar said we could come to your ceilidhe, only first we must go to sleep. Do you mind?"

"There's only one I'd as soon have," replied Brogeen. "And she's dancing through the streets of the Cake Town in the green shoes. But who said I was giving a ceilidhe?"

"You're not giving a ceilidhe! Your friends are giving one to welcome you home!" explained Jim. "Jump in now! There isn't much time!"

Brogeen scrambled in beside the parcels.

"Allow me!" neighed the phouka, politely, and gave a push with his head which sent the wheelbarrow rolling along the boreen.

Jim and Judy raced along the road, laughing and calling out—

"Brogeen's home! Brogeen's home!"

From every bush came excited chirps and flutters. Up and down the boreen the neighbours were twittering.

> "Welcome home, Brogeen!
> Where have you been?
> What have you seen?
> We missed you, Brogeen!
> Swallows are gone.

There's not much song.
Nights are long.
We're glad you've come—
Welcome home, Brogeen!"

Brogeen sat up very straight. He clutched the sides of the wheelbarrow and felt his face, even his ears, growing redder and redder.

"When they see me in the light, I'll be ashamed! Me clothes is wore out! I'm just a bundle of rags! What'll I do at all?"

As they rolled past the rushes, the frog poked out his head

"Ye're back, adventurer!" he called, and splashed down, only to pop up again. "I'll be seeing ye!"

Across the stepping stones the phouka stood still. Brogeen's door was wide open and he could see inside. A fire burned on the hearth and a lighted lantern hung from the roof.

As he watched, the Woman of the Roads put his little kettle near the blaze, then came towards him.

"Welcome home, Brogeen! Listen now, go in and look in your chest. Mrs MacDonald's made you a new suit. And Judy knitted the red cap and the muffler. They couldn't make shoes. No one can make shoes like you,

Brogeen! We'll be back for the ceilidhe!"

And off she went, clinging to the tail of the phouka.

There were lanterns hanging in all the roots of the beech tree. There were scurryings and bumps and whisperings. But Brogeen knew he mustn't look—yet!

He stepped inside and closed the door. His little brown teapot was hot. His blue cup and saucer were ready on the table. He looked at the loaded wheelbarrow and began to unwrap the parcels. In the middle he stopped and opened the chest.

There lay his new suit, with the red muffler and the long cap. But the chest looked empty without the green shoes until he laid his bag of tools inside.

"There's the ceilidhe tonight, and me friends to meet, and me story to tell!" he thought. "Wisha! 'Tis a long story!"

The kettle began to sing—

WELCOME HOME, BROGEEN!

Children's
POOLBEG

The Turf Cutter's Donkey

and

Brogeen Follows the
Magic Tune

by

Patricia Lynch

"Classics of Irish Children's Literature"

Irish Independent

£2.99

Children's
POOLBEG

Orla Was Six
  Mary Beckett   £2.99
Candy on the Dart
  Ita Daly   £2.99
*When the Luvenders
  Came to Merrick Town*
  June Considine   £3.50
Discoveries
  Clodagh Corcoran ed   £4.99
Baker's Dozen
  Clodagh Corcoran ed   £3.50
Children's Quiz Book No. 1
  Robert Duffy   £2.99
Children's Quiz Book No. 2
  Robert Duffy   £2.99
Joe in the Middle
  Tony Hickey   £2.99
Where is Joe?
  Tony Hickey   £3.50
Spike and the Professor
  Tony Hickey   £2.99
Blanketland
  Tony Hickey   £2.99
The Bridge of Feathers
  Eamon Kelly   £2.99
The Turf-Cutter's Donkey
  Patricia Lynch   £2.99
*Brogeen Follows the
  Magic Tune*
  Patricia Lynch   £2.99

*Brogeen and the Green
  Shoes*
  Patricia Lynch   £3.50
Patsy-O
  Bryan MacMahon   £2.99
Growing Things
  Sean McCann   £2.99
*Shoes and Ships and
  Sealing-Wax*
  A Book of Quotations for Children
  Sean McMahon ed   £2.99
*The Poolbeg Book of
  Children's Verse*
  Sean McMahon ed   £4.95
The Viking Princess
  Michael Mullen   £2.99
The Little Drummer Boy
  Michael Mullen   £2.99
The Little Black Hen
  Eileen O'Faoláin   £2.99
An Nollaig Thiar
  Breandán Ó hEithir   £2.99
Bugsy Goes to Limerick
  Carolyn Swift   £2.99
Robbers on TV
  Carolyn Swift   £2.99
A Little Man in England
  Shaun Traynor   £2.99
Hugo O'Huge
  Shaun Traynor   £2.99